BBC

DOCTOR WHO

STAR TALES

BBC

DOCTOR WHO
STAR TALES

Trevor Baxendale, Steve Cole,
Jenny T. Colgan, Jo Cotterill,
Paul Magrs and Mike Tucker

BBC
BOOKS

1 3 5 7 9 10 8 6 4 2

BBC Books, an imprint of Ebury Publishing
20 Vauxhall Bridge Road,
London SW1V 2SA

BBC Books is part of the Penguin Random House group of companies whose addresses can be found at global.penguinrandomhouse.com

Penguin Random House UK

First published by BBC Books in 2019

www.eburypublishing.co.uk

A CIP catalogue record for this book is available from the British Library

ISBN 9781785944710

Editorial Director: Albert DePetrillo
Project Editor: Steve Cole
Cover design: Lee Binding © Woodland Books Ltd, 2019
Production: Sian Pratley

A man called John Cox and his Houdini website https://www.wildabouthoudini.com were very helpful with Houdini research.

Typeset in 13.7/17.3 pt ITC Albertina MT Std
by Integra Software Services Pvt. Ltd, Pondicherry

Printed and bound in Great Britain by Clays Ltd, Elcograf S.p.A.

Contents

Chasing the Dawn

Jenny T. Colgan

Yaz walked quickly to the door leading from the console room. Time was of the essence. 'Doctor?' she yelled.

'Why do you need her?' said Graham, looking up from the console. 'Can't we help?'

'No reason,' said Yaz quickly, as Ryan glanced across at her. There was an awkward pause, then she walked away.

'Doctor?' Yaz found her fiddling with wires that were spilling out of a panel on a distant wall, wearing her goggles. 'Um, are you busy?' she said.

The Doctor pulled up her goggles. 'For you, Yaz, never.'

The wires sparked and one briefly caught fire. Yaz looked at it pointedly as the Doctor shot her hand quickly behind her back and pinched it out without looking.

'So ...?'

'I need ...' Yaz frowned. She'd thought several times about what would be a good way to approach this, and hadn't come up with anything so far. 'It's ... well. It's my time of the month, and ...'

The Doctor grinned. 'I have just the thing. Four things in fact.'

Yaz squinted. 'Just ... the usual will probably be fine ...'

'Noooo' said the Doctor. 'Come with me.'

Yaz followed, smiling.

'I've travelled with a lot of human females,' said the Doctor intriguingly.

'Have you?' said Yaz, interested.

'Follow me …' The Doctor screwed up her face. 'Ah yes. Hungarian bathroom …'

They set off rapidly down the endless corridors, Yaz looking around worriedly. Getting lost in here haunted her dreams, even if the determined person walking quickly beside her would never let her get lost. She knew that.

The Doctor hardly ever mentioned people she'd travelled with in the past. Yaz wondered; had there been many? Hundreds? What had happened to them all?

The Hungarian bathroom had been quite something, its rococo detailing something to be dwelt on and admired. Yaz wondered who cleaned the whirlpool bath, with its gleaming golden chains.

'Thanks,' she said, emerging.

'OK! Next!' said the Doctor, who was outside the door, staring at a fish tank on the opposite wall she'd completely forgotten was there. The fish, though, appeared to be thriving. She opened a random cupboard door, took out a hot water bottle and handed it to Yaz.

It was, Yaz was both surprised and unsurprised to note, already hot.

Then followed a very long walk down a seemingly endless spiral staircase, that brought them to a pair of very tall gates. Yaz stared at them, astonished, as the Doctor opened them.

'What's behind there?' she asked, as the Doctor slipped between them.

'Sorry,' said the Doctor airily, closing the high gate behind her. 'Nobody ever goes out and nobody ever comes in.' She returned with a vast bar of the most delicious, creamy-tasting chocolate Yaz had ever known.

'OK,' conceded Yaz. 'So you do know a lot of human females.'

The Doctor frowned slightly. 'It's easier looking like this.'

'Blonde?'

'Like a girl.'

'Oh. OH. Don't you always?'

'Nope.'

'Is that weird?'

'I have,' said the Doctor grandly, 'quite a lot of bandwidth for weird.'

Yaz bit her lip. 'OK. Does it matter what you look like?'

'Sometimes,' said the Doctor. 'You didn't ask me what the fourth thing was.'

'Oh yes,' said Yaz.

They had gotten themselves comfortably ensconced on a nearby chaise longue. The Doctor pulled her knees up to her chest.

'A story!' she announced. 'Would you like one?'

Yaz settled back into the deep purple cushions of the incredibly comfortable squishy sofa, put the hot water bottle on her tummy and opened the chocolate. 'Oh! So much …'

The engine was making a peculiar juddering noise, and there was wind whistling through various gaps in the fuselage, but Amelia Jane Earhart was used to that. Anything lower than a high-pitched squeal in the engines was always fixable. Sometimes just with a good knock with a wrench. That was flying machines for you.

'Noonan?'

Her navigator was taking a snooze in the back of the tiny fuselage, surrounded by spare fuel and supplies. Even though the engine noise was deafening, he was snoring peacefully. Amelia grinned. Typical sprocket. They had all learned to grab forty winks when they could.

She moved forwards and looked out of the tiny front window of the Electra. The view was of pale blue sky and pale blue water, both of them indistinguishable apart from the slim line of white curving round the horizon.

Despite the enduring noise of the plane and the clicking of the joystick, Amelia felt as she always did: completely at peace; soaring above the grubby world below, with its endless fundraising and jockeying for sponsors and publicity, and flashbulb cameras in her faces, and newspapermen shouting – men, everywhere, telling her off and doubting her credentials. Here, with a light hand on the joystick, her short hair tucked neatly behind her ears, the only man within a thousand miles fast asleep, and her plane responding perfectly in her hands; here, soaring above the world, only a tiny splash in the water six hundred feet below – a whale? A shark? – the sole evidence that she wasn't completely alone in the universe. Here and here alone, Earhart's spirit calmed and she felt, simultaneously, both at home and utterly free. She smiled to herself, and checked the instruments. She was approaching the International Date Line: longitude 180 degrees exactly, where she would run two days twice. She'd have to remember that in the log. But for now they were steady as she—

Two things happened very quickly.

First, she thought she saw something, a long way off, almost certainly a trick of the light, but it looked like something hanging in the air – not a bird, not a cloud. She screwed her eyes up, just as, suddenly, they appeared to be flying through a thin purple line, hanging in the sky, as if a rope had been thrown down from a cloud. Except the line *hummed*. There was ... something. Above the noise of the engines, came a great buzz, as if a sudden plague of insects or locusts was passing through the entire cabin, as well as an extraordinary rushing sound.

And then it was gone.

She looked all around, but could see nothing where the line had been. She frowned and reached for the logbook.

She heard a strange gurgling sound right behind her.

'Noonan? Fred?'

The gurgle turned into a strained yelping noise.

Amelia clicked on the brand new Sperry autopilot and scrambled out to the back.

Amelia Jane Earhart was not a cowardly person. On the contrary, she was one of the bravest people in the world.

But what she saw in the back of the plane made her shrink back in terror and start to shake.

The Doctor was swinging gently from his hammock, hanging from the TARDIS on the very cusp of the International Date Line. A tall man in a tweed jacket and black trousers, he looked like a young man assembled by old men from memory.

The Panama hat he was wearing was slightly too small for him, which was irritating, but his book was good, which made him happy, after he had been to all the trouble of hanging the hammock. Especially after the swing debacle.

It also tickled him to be in a place where there was nothing definite to do, just the pale blue of the sea below him and the light turquoise of the sky above him and …

The tiny biplane seemed to appear out of absolutely nowhere, blundering through the sky, bouncing, rearing up, then tearing between him and the TARDIS above, smoke puffing out of its tail, putt-putting ahead.

'Golly,' said the Doctor. His hat fell off his head onto his book, and he stared at the plane crossly as it spun around, doing loop the loops. 'Showing off,' he added. 'I like showing off.'

He quickly shinned up the hammock sides and scrambled back inside the TARDIS to see what was up.

Amelia was still staring in horror at the prone figure of Noonan on the bottom of the aircraft. What could possibly have caused this?

The plane started to buck without her at the controls, and she braced herself against its metal framework to try and work out what to do next.

Noonan's face was pulled back in a hideous rictus grin. His teeth were exposed, his gums a ghastly green colour, as were his eye sockets – wide, red rimmed, already rotting. He looked like a corpse that had been there for a long time. But even as she looked at him he twitched; twitched again. Not like a person, but as if something was moving him from the inside. Crawling beneath his skin, a livid green trail up and down his pale empty flesh. Getting closer.

Amelia was not the screaming type.

The Electra was though, and now she was starting to make a very uncomfortable set of noises.

'A race, huh?' said the Doctor, watching the little plane bounce along the warm air currents. 'Always!' And he jammed the TARDIS into gear, meaning it immediately toppled sideways, which at least sorted out the hat problem.

He felt wistful for a moment. He was on his own. Nothing fun was quite as much fun on your own.

Then he did a speedy handbrake turn and shot off into the bright blue horizon in pursuit of the tumbling plane.

Amelia clicked off the automatic pilot, whereupon the plane immediately rolled. Her heart was pounding. What had happened to Noonan?

She couldn't think about that now; she had a plane to right. Oh God, why was everything so blue? As the plane tumbled, it was impossible to tell which way was up; what was water and what was sky. She screwed up her eyes and could just about … Was that a spit of gold ahead, a tiny blip in the ocean? Was it an optical illusion, or could it be land?

She was suddenly distracted to her left as something came pummelling out of the air towards her: a strange, square box, on its side, a blue light at the front of it leading on. It was quite spectacularly non-aerodynamic.

She blinked. It must be an airship. Surely not the newspapermen again? And how on earth was it moving so fast? As she stared at it, a door flopped open from top to bottom, and a large-faced man poked his head out and waved cheerily.

She frowned back at him. What was this? A newspaper stunt? A rival? And why were there always men trying to prove her wrong? She grimaced back at him, then turned back to the matter on hand: could she land on the tiny spit? Or should she carry on, try and get Noonan to Howland Island, where there would be medical facilities on the ships.

Then the noise came: a rustling, shaking, dreadful noise. It was liquid, a thick sound, like something moving beneath skin. Amelia couldn't believe it, after what she'd seen. Was Noonan still alive?

'Fred?' she said plaintively. But those eyes, that rotting, churning flesh. Even the smell had started to seep through over the normally overpowering scent of gasoline.

The cracking noise came again, as well as a horrible thud.

Something, which had once been Fred, was on the move.

'Oh come on!' said the Doctor, still trying to get the woman's attention. 'I just want to race.'

He gracefully clambered back inside, and wound the TARDIS around and up and over the little plane again.

See, he said to himself, mutinously. You couldn't do this when other people were there. They kept falling over and complaining about not wanting to fall over, and elbows and things. He could do whatever he liked, by himself. So there.

He sat on the wall – now the floor – of the TARDIS and let her glide along, making beckoning noises to the other plane. As he looked up, he saw the other plane suddenly making a swift dive.

He immediately followed.

It was the shape of Fred. It looked like Fred. But it wasn't. The body rippled and pulsed in strange ways; the eyes were pallid. Bits of flesh were erupting from what looked like the outside in. Even over the incredibly strong smell of fuel, the stink was absolutely ungodly.

'Oh my God,' said Amelia. The figure lurched towards her. Whatever it was, whatever was happening, she knew somehow, with every fibre of her being, that she couldn't let it touch her. 'Get back!'

The thing that used to be Fred howled weirdly, a creaking, guttering noise that sounded like something running over his voice box.

'Stay away!'

It lurched forwards with the plane, reaching out a green clammy hand to her shoulder.

She leapt back and glanced around. Could she make it to open the aircraft door? It was a two-handed twist which would take about five seconds. And they were dropping out of the sky at a rate of knots. She looked down at her hands and willed them to stop shaking. She had been in worse situations than this. Well, maybe not worse.

She pulled out her zippo lighter from her pocket, then put it away again. The figure might be scared of fire, but the entire plane must be covered in gasoline. They'd both go up.

Instead, Amelia lifted her large boot and kicked out at the creature, sending it hurling back towards the very back of the aircraft, buying herself crucial seconds.

She pulled up the nose, looked at the instruments and down into the blue. The spit of yellow sand was clearer now. She could ... if she set the angle just right ... if she could run and open the door and throw that *thing*, which even now she could hear getting up, groaning, creaking, the ligaments twisting around themselves ... if she could throw it out ... and land the plane ...

She glanced to her left. That absolute idiot was still leaning out of the blue airship, waving wildly and mouthing 'HALLLOOOOOO!!!!' but she didn't have time to think about that just now.

She very carefully propped the joystick up, just a tad, and engaged the autopilot once more. She could hear the thing now – it wasn't breathing, but making rasping noises as it moved, as if something was moving its throat.

She whisked around. The creature was worse now, if anything: more and more holes appearing as its skin integrity broke down. The whole thing was pulsing with motion, with whatever was inside, but it was slow-moving.

Amelia ducked under its arm and dived to the doorway, pulling at the handle and turning it round until it fell open. The air outside was warm at the lowering altitude, the noise formidable, roaring past her ears. The pale turquoise sea looked uncomfortably close.

She turned. She fastened her gloves more tightly. She didn't want it touching her flesh. Looking round, she grabbed the largest thing she could find – the axe, for cutting chocks. She hoisted it, keeping her balance in the stuttering plane as they headed ever downwards.

Then she rushed at the creature, chopping with the axe just above Fred's boots. The thing lurched over, and she grabbed at its hand, which came off in her glove. Amelia squealed in disgust, then swallowed hard, and seized the remaining piece of arm, swinging the creature round to use its weight against it, and hurling it downwards with all her might. Then she sent the arm after it, even as the plane lurched and half her supplies fell out too.

The Doctor watched in dismay as the figure fell from the aircraft. What had happened?

The TARDIS dived and materialised directly beneath the plummeting figure, outlined sharply against the pale blue of the sky. The figure plopped through the upturned open door of the TARDIS, followed by several clumsy tanks of petroleum tumbling in its wake.

The Doctor looked on, horrified, as they plunged past him into the depths of the ship and exploded. 'Do *not* make me replace the armoire again!'

There was a second, louder explosion. The Doctor closed his eyes and made a faint moue of disappointment.

Amelia turned away. She didn't have the luxury of speculation; she had a plane to land.

The joystick rattled the teeth in her mouth, but opening the cargo door had slowed the descent further. The spit of land was smaller than she'd hoped: it couldn't be more than a hundred yards long, a featureless pop of sand in an otherwise vast and empty ocean.

She could carry on, but there was no land due and she'd lost a lot of fuel when she'd got rid of … whatever Noonan had become. No. She would have to land and take stock and sort everything out. Without a navigator, she could certainly get herself home, but it would be tricky.

She pulled the plane into circles, gradually descending to give herself the best possible chance of being able to get out on dry land rather than ditching into the sea. Focusing her eyes on the spit, she came down … slowly, slowly … attempted a landing, muffed it and pulled up again.

The Doctor put off investigating the mess downstairs and settled back to watch the plane instead, admiring the pilot's skill with the beautiful silver bird. It swooped round in lower and lower parabolas, the vapour trail knotting behind it like weaving as it finally, gently spluttered down, rolling, rolling, all the way to the end of the tiny islet, the wheels coming to a halt mere centimetres from the pale blue waves.

'I say, bravo, *bravo,*' he said, quickly landing the TARDIS, bounding out joyfully and applauding as Amelia clambered down from the cockpit, taking off her helmet and frowning. 'Beautiful work.'

Amelia turned round crossly. If he was a journalist ... 'Who the *hell*—'

They both froze. Out of the door the Doctor had carelessly left ajar came a figure – swirling, retching, moving jerkily; burned black yet somehow still slowly progressing.

'Fascinating,' breathed the Doctor.

'*Kill it!*' screamed Amelia. She glanced around for anything to hand, ran back to the plane and grabbed a large tin of fuel. 'For pity's sake, let him die!' She opened the screw top, ran up and hurled it at the figure of Noonan.

She and the Doctor threw themselves to the ground. By the time she'd uncovered her ears from the almighty blast, and dared to look up, there was clearing smoke, and black marks on the sand ... but no sign of the monster that had once been her navigator and her friend.

She stood up, very, very slowly, looking all around. The spit of sand was about 200 yards long and 50 yards wide. Apart from that, and the ridiculous journalist and his ridiculous airship, there was nothing to be seen but endless water and endless sky and, suddenly, a deep, extraordinary silence. Not a bird's cry to disturb the peace; not even the faintest lapping against the shore. It was, in its own way, very beautiful.

'So *hallo there*!' came the voice.

*

'I'm not sure she's going to like you,' said Yaz, hugging the hot water bottle – which, pleasingly, didn't appear to go cold – closer to her stomach.

The Doctor sighed. 'I know. Do you think she'd have liked me more like this?'

Yaz nodded wholeheartedly. 'Of course! You could have shared so much. Two flying women! With their own ships! That would have been amazing!'

'It would have, wouldn't it?' The Doctor looked into the middle distance. 'We could have flown together. Gone anywhere. She was so brave, such a pioneer . . .'

Her voice went a little hoarse.

'So of course I managed to completely stuff it up.'

'Don't you look terrific! *Lovely* tin can thing! I mean, it has wings and it's pointy, but you can't have everything . . .'

Amelia stalked over to the tall character with the bow tie who seemed unable to stop talking. 'Who the hell are you?'

'Ah. I'm the Doctor. Hello. Such a thrill to meet you, Miss Earhart.'

She rolled her eyes. 'Amelia is fine.'

'Splendid! I really, really like Amelias!'

'Which newspaper are you from?'

'Which *newspaper*?' The Doctor considered for a moment. '*The Daily Planet*,' he announced with confidence. 'So can you tell me what happened?'

Amelia walked slowly to where the explosion had happened. Black streaks still ran across the ground. She shook her head in disbelief. 'No. Noonan . . . one moment he was . . . it was like something took him over.'

The Doctor came up behind her, knelt down and took out a strange flashlight which he proceeded to point at the black traces. The device made a beeping noise, and he immediately jumped up. 'Stand back,' he barked.

Amelia normally never listened to anyone but something in the tone of his voice made her obey, for once. And also what had happened to Noonan was terrifying. There was no point taking unnecessary risks.

'What is it?' she said.

'Did you touch him?'

She held up her flying gloves. 'Only with these.'

The Doctor glanced up, looked at Amelia and scanned her with his flashlight. 'OK, then. Good.'

She took off her goggles and squinted at him. 'But what ...'

The Doctor heaved a sigh.

Amelia gave a final glance at the last traces of Noonan, then turned round and headed back to her plane to see if it was damaged. The Doctor walked with her.

'You know where we are?'

'The International Date Line.'

'That's right. A hairline crack in time.'

'But it's imaginary!'

'All time is imaginary,' said the Doctor self-importantly. 'But some is more imaginary than others.'

'Is it?' asked Yaz.

'Yes,' said the Doctor. 'But I shouldn't have told her. I was just showing off.'

*

Amelia gave him a long hard look. You met more than a few cranks when you were one of the most famous women in the world. 'Oh, good,' she said wearily.

'So anyway,' said the Doctor, bouncing next to her on his long legs. 'There is a crack. A tiny, hair-thin line. Between one day and the next, or the day after. And it's here. Good place to slip through undetected.'

Amelia looked at him. 'For what to slip through?'

'Well, what did you see?'

'I ...' Amelia took off her flying cap – it was warm – and screwed up her eyes, trying to make sense of it. 'It's like ... there was a line. A thin purple line. And then it was like he was covered in bugs. Under his skin. But he can't have been ...'

'Forget about what can't have been,' said the Doctor.

'Shush, I'm thinking,' said Amelia.

The Doctor pursed his lips in slightly hurt silence as Amelia went on.

'It was as if his skin was pulsing, mutating ... Could it have been a parasite of some kind? Picked up on Hawaii?' Amelia blinked and went on. 'But acting so rapidly ... I've never seen anything like it before ... Perhaps the altitude brought it on, made it develop? But how does it move from host to host? If it kills the victim so quickly ...'

'He didn't die,' the Doctor pointed out. 'We had to blow him up.'

'But I saw his eyes ... His eyes were dead.'

'They can feed,' said the Doctor. 'For a very long time.'

'You know what they are?'

The Doctor pulled a face. 'Maybe.'

'Did you bring them?'

'No! No, no, no.' The Doctor shook his head vehemently. 'They must have found the same loophole I did ...'

'Loophole from where?'

'Could be Chriousian ... Felp has some pretty nasty bug life.' He looked at her and then turned round proudly. 'It wasn't me. My ship has automatic quarantine!'

'You look like you just walked out of Brooks Brothers,' said Amelia, narrowing her eyes. 'How d'ya fly so clean?'

'I won't stay clean for long,' said the Doctor. 'I need to examine your plane.'

'What if I don't want you anywhere near my plane?'

'What if there's one of those bugs left?'

Amelia thought again about Noonan's blank staring eyes. 'But you're a journalist.'

'Exactly!' said the Doctor gleefully. '*Excellent* with lowlife and things that crawl across the ground!'

The tyres were burst, and the landing gear needed work but, on the whole, things could have been a lot worse. That was true of the body of the plane, at least. The fuel on the other hand was a different matter. Rather a lot of it had gone. Amelia sighed.

She looked at the strange man suspiciously. He was crawling on his hands and knees with his flashlight peering into every nook and cranny, turning his head upside down.

'I think,' he said. 'I think we might have been lucky. I think your poor friend copped it all.'

'What does your plane run on?' Amelia said, straightening up and staring through the cabin door at the strange box. It was the least aerodynamic thing she'd ever seen; she really couldn't work it out at all.

'Um ... stuff,' said the Doctor.

Amelia folded her arms. Men assuming that she didn't understand technical terms was one of her least favourite things. 'Gasoline?' she asked.

'Noooo! Although I do have a fondue set in there ... somewhere ...'

Amelia frowned. 'What do you run on, then? Is it an airship?'

'Um, kind of.'

'Hydrogen won't work for me,' said Amelia to herself. 'Well, that's the kiss-off. Noonan lost and my plane ditched.'

She counted up the number of barrels of gasoline left, then pulled out the map, working out the sums with a pencil. 'Can't go forward, can't go back,' she said eventually.

The sun was hot on her back and she was thirsty. There was no fresh water on the islet at all. When she turned round, however, she thought it was a mirage: the Doctor appeared to be drinking a cup of hot tea in a china cup and saucer.

'Tea?' he said, and irritatingly she felt compelled to agree.

They sat cross-legged in the sand, Amelia thinking quickly about how to get out of there, the Doctor keeping his eyes on the sand, everywhere. He had a shrewd idea of what the parasites were, and he wasn't going anywhere until he'd made absolutely sure nothing was still about.

Amelia regarded the water, as the Doctor disappeared into his ship once more. 'Is it just me?' she hollered after him. 'Or is the tide coming in?'

'Oh yes,' said the Doctor, reappearing with a fresh pot of tea and, rather disappointingly, for him at least, a packet of bourbons. 'It does that.'

Amelia jumped up and turned around. 'On all sides!' she said. 'This island is going to vanish.'

The Doctor nodded. 'These things do come and go ...'

'But my plane ...' Amelia swore and bit into the bourbon biscuit. 'Actually, this is good.'

'No, it's *awful*.' The Doctor hurled his biscuit crossly into the encroaching surf.

'What have you got against bourbons?' asked Yaz.

'Well, if it's not obvious, I don't know how I could possibly explain,' said the Doctor huffily, suddenly sounding quite unlike herself. Yaz glanced at her, but the Doctor's face was lost in the past.

'So you have cookies but no gasoline? Oh well. I couldn't make it alone anyway.' Amelia slumped down in the sand. 'Guess that dream is over. Plenty of good ol' boys back at the USPA will be pleased.'

The Doctor eyed the plane critically. 'I expect ...' he said. 'I expect my ship could tow your ship.'

Amelia snorted. 'As if that's ever happened. Pulled along by some Joe.' She got up, shook the sand off her jodhpurs and started changing the tyres on the Electra.

There wasn't much point, she knew, but she had to do something.

The sun shone steadily. Amelia had taken off her heavy jacket under its bright glare. She kept the goggles on. Meanwhile the strange man was pacing the shoreline shining his flashlight. It was distracting.

'What are you doing?'

'Just checking,' said the Doctor. 'I don't … What was inside your friend … They're blooming resilient. Remember the influenza?'

Amelia sat back on her haunches and nodded. Of course she did. It had wiped out half the world, it felt like. She'd been a nurse in those days, had watched the young men come back from the war, then fade away. She had never forgotten it.

'That. But faster. We can't risk any of it getting free.'

'So I'd not just be a woman ruining airplanes for men, I'd also destroy the entire world by bringing back a plague.' She gave him a level look. 'Quite the headline.'

'You're changing everything, you know,' he said gently. 'You open up the world. Especially for women. For everyone. To travel.'

'I guess you read tea leaves, huh?' Amelia looked ruefully at the plane. 'I wanted to change things. So much. But, now …'

'Whether you succeed or not,' the Doctor began, looking away. Then he stopped. 'Get back!'

It was under the chocks of the wheels. About the size of a thumb; purplish, like a writhing bruise. Clearly in its death agonies. Clearly not dead yet.

The Doctor took out a handkerchief and lifted it. Amelia backed away, disgusted and horrified at the same time. It was beautiful, but …

'Well, hello,' said the Doctor, examining it carefully. 'Aren't you pretty for such a deadly thing …'

The thing bounced out of his hand and exploded in mid-air.

'What?'

Amelia was brushing her hands down on her trousers. The stone that had hit the creature had tumbled down to the ground.

'What did you *do*?'

'Put it out of its misery,' said Amelia.

The Doctor bent down. The thing was quite dead. He pulled out his flashlight and pressed on it. 'Losiruz,' he said. 'Thought so.'

'The influenza?'

'The influenza, yes,' said the Doctor sadly. He rummaged in his pocket and brought out a box of matches, trying and failing to light them in the sea breeze. Amelia threw him her zippo. He knelt down, carefully made a small mound for the creature, surrounded by stones, and set it on fire. 'Just to be safe.' He stood up respectfully and bowed his head. 'It's just an animal, you know. Doing what all animals are designed to do.'

'Survive?'

'Explore,' said the Doctor, giving her a look.

The entire sky was pink by the time he had finished examining every grain of sand. The water was lapping right up to their boots; the wheels of the plane were nearly underneath.

Amelia had counted and recounted the fuel. She had spread out the maps on the sand. It was impossible, and she knew it, and she was going to have to swallow her pride.

'Can you really tow me?' she said. 'Just to the nearest port.'

'Sure can,' said the Doctor. 'Can untether you in mid air, if you like. You don't even need to tell them I was here.'

Amelia stared at him. 'Tell a lot of lies, do you?'

'Did you really think she could make it? Didn't you think it would… change the history of the world or something?'

'Not really,' said the Doctor, looking shifty. 'It wasn't a fixed point in time or anything.'

'But she didn't make it,' said Yaz.

'No,' said the Doctor, very slowly. 'Well, anyway, shall we get back to the others?'

'No!'

'Blimey, you're snappy.'

'Don't start.'

'Right,' said the Doctor. 'Let's get the Electra tied up.' He had brought out the hammock, which was strong enough to hold anything.

Amelia face fell and she felt icy cold all of a sudden. Why had she listened to him? Why had she believed he could take her plane?

'You have a *hammock* in there? And *no gasoline?*'

'I'll stick it on the list,' grunted the Doctor as he marched over to the plane.

A larger than normal wave washed over what was left of the tiny spit. Amelia jumped as it splashed her face. 'This is ridiculous!' she said, white with fury. 'You can't tow a plane with a hammock! It's crazy!'

'Time to go,' said the Doctor, just as a much larger wave broke over the other side of the spit. They were both up to their ankles now. 'No need to panic. It's Dalrussian filament . . .'

Amelia looked around the bright purple sky; the thousand miles of nothing but water in every single direction. 'Time to go,' she said, suddenly calm, just as a large wave slapped the other side of the islet. This time, instead of receding, the wave started to pull the sand with it. The plane inexorably started to move and – even though she knew it was irrational, even though she knew it couldn't help matters – Amelia couldn't bear it. 'The Electra!' she shouted, tearing away.

'No!' shouted the Doctor. 'No! Don't! It's not safe! Just give me two minutes! Wait!'

He was tying one end of the hammock to the doorknob of the TARDIS. Amelia turned round, briefly, eyes shining, and looked at him as if this was the single stupidest thing she had ever seen.

'I am *so fed up*,' she said, 'of being told what to do.'

With two bounds, she was by the cockpit door, which was already slanting horribly to one side.

'Nooo!' The Doctor charged after her, trailing the hammock, trying to throw it over the tail of the plane as Amelia deftly kicked away the chocks, pulled down the propeller once, twice until it started up, then vaulted into the cockpit, pulling down her googles.

'If I found one spit of land, I can find another!' she yelled. 'You go fetch me my damn gasoline. I'll meet you there. I am *not* giving up.'

The Doctor attached the hammock to the end of the tail even as the plane started to move, wheels jerking through the water. It was up to his knees now. He sadly started splashing back to the TARDIS. Surely the weight of the water would hold her back, and keep her down? And there was only a hundred metres or so of beach – she'd never make it. He stood near the door of the TARDIS, ready to go and fetch her if she tipped into the waves.

But he had underestimated the willpower and skill of the young woman. The plane gathered speed, splashing, stuttering and choking. As the sky turned bright gold and pink and the shadow flickered across the endless water, the plane balked, spluttered – and finally, miraculously, lifted across the shining sea, heading east, the sun sending out its dying rays behind it. Darkness was spreading ahead, and the plane looked tiny as it headed into the wide blue sky.

The Doctor took off his hat and watched in admiration. Then he ran back to the TARDIS, grabbing the hammock as he went. He planned, of course, to follow her. But discreetly this time.

'I should have … She should have come with me,' said the Doctor fiercely.

'Well, what were you going to do, knock her over the head and carry her into the TARDIS?' said Yaz, trying to be comforting.

'Never was my style. But if ...' She put her hands on her hair. 'Oh I don't know. She'd fought with her father; with every other flyer. I can't help but wonder if I'd looked a bit more like this ... Well. Who knows. She flew all through the night.'

'Did you watch her? I can't imagine you staying still for that long.'

There was a long silence. The Doctor looked down at her legs, remembering a longer pair, dangling out of the TARDIS on a tropical night, warm, silent, like a velvet cocoon, the stars popping out like heavy strands of twinkling diamonds.

'I did,' she said. 'I kept my distance. She didn't look for me once.'

'But she must have known she couldn't keep going forever.'

'She did.'

Amelia felt the ridiculousness of the situation. It was dark. The moon was full, so she could see the lapping waves beneath her but nothing that remotely looked like land. There was no land on the map for another thousand miles. She had fuel for – she looked at her calculations again. Another 323 miles. No matter how she parsed the numbers or slowed down the engine. It would come to the same thing in the end: she'd have to ditch. What if he couldn't land? Or get to her? He didn't have a co-pilot as far as she could see.

The radio crackled into life above the steady roar of the engine. 'Hallo? Hallo!'

Amelia rolled her eyes. But what could she do? 'This is Electra. Over,' she said.

'Ooh! This is TARDIS! That's the name of my ship. Except I don't call her that. I call her ... Anyway, it's me. Over!'

'Yes, I gathered.' Nonetheless, she decided, she was glad he was there. 'We're doing just fine here, TARDIS. Just chasing the dawn. Over.'

'I realise that. I'm so glad to hear your voice! I still have the hammock …'

Amelia gritted her teeth. 'Like I said, Electra is doing just fine, thank you.'

'Well, any time you want to come on board … I have cake …'

'Fine for cake, thank you. Over and out.'

Amelia concentrated. On the horizon there was the simplest line of brightest gold, a tiny hint. Around her there was stillness, the black shifting to the darkest of blues. She would keep going, she resolved. Just the tiniest bit of land. She wasn't asking much. Somewhere, anywhere. The maps didn't show every inch of the ocean. She'd found one spit. She could find another.

Her eyes strained along the endless dark blue water, beginning to lighten at the very eastern reaches into palest turquoise. Somewhere ahead – it could have been five miles, or fifty – another large animal crested the water, bounced and splashed and turned again, oblivious to the two strange ships in the sky above it; caring even less if it had seen them as the drone moved on.

The fuel gauge was slipping, and Amelia kept found herself drifting off at the controls, that strange, falling-up-a-step feeling when your brain thought it was awake and found to its surprise that it was not. But she had to go on. She had to carry on. There had to be land. There had to be.

She opened the radio. 'Calling TAR—'

'I'm here! Yes! I'm here! Hallo!'

'How fast can your airplane travel?'

'*Dead fast!*'

'Do you think . . .' She sighed and looked at the gauge again. 'Do you think you might go and fetch me some gasoline now?'

There was a long pause.

'No,' came the voice, and it sounded, suddenly, dreadfully sad.

'Why not?' said Yaz, sitting up crossly. 'Why didn't you just go?'

'Two reasons, both rubbish,' the Doctor said ruefully. 'One, if I went, but at appropriate speed, I'd leave her alone for too long. I knew exactly how much fuel she had. She'd have ditched. And two, if I went and looped in time to return immediately . . . Well, I already knew we were being watched. That there were parasites around, not from Earth; waiting. Waiting for a point to slip through. If I'd messed with time just then . . .'

'They'd have made it?'

'The universe makes holes all the time,' said the Doctor. 'But when there are wolves nearby, you hammer the doors shut. You hammer them tight.'

'OK then,' said Amelia, and she sounded so weary. 'Can you go on ahead and see if there's any land? Even a small amount?'

'There isn't.'

'How do you know that?'

'I just do. Let me tow you. Please.'

Amelia looked at the instruments. The diminishing fuel tank. The place behind her, where Noonan should have been. She had to be honest with herself. She wasn't going to make it, and she hadn't been ever since she'd touched down. The reason she was so hostile to this stranger was he was her only hope of getting out of there. And having to rely on someone was absolutely the opposite of the reason why she'd made this trip in the first place.

She sighed heavily. 'You really think you can do it in that ship?'

'I do, yes.'

Amelia turned as far as the cockpit windows would let her see in all directions. The colours of the dawn were now bright all around her, bright wild purples and pinks that made her feel as if she was inside a kaleidoscope. It was so beautiful, it didn't feel threatening. But it was. The world was hers and hers alone … for just a few moments more.

She took a deep breath. 'OK,' she said. 'What do you need me to do?'

'Nothing!' said the Doctor cheerfully. 'Well. Catch this.'

He parked the TARDIS just beside the little plane, close enough to throw the netting to Amelia, who propped the plane and opened the cabin door. She teetered in the open door as the wind blew past them both and the fuel needle bumped along, close to empty. The netting of the hammock, though, was made of a curious material she didn't recognise, and it felt as strong as steel.

The Doctor put two thumbs up. 'Stick it under the fuselage, and let it jam on the wheels! Then you can just glide!' he yelled over the radio. 'All the way to—'

'—Howland,' finished Amelia glumly. 'I don't think my sponsors will be too impressed at me getting a tow.'

'Oh, it's only money.'

'Only people with money ever say that!'

The engine was stuttering, closer now. She'd left it to the very last minute. There was barely another drop in the tanks.

They started to drift downwards.

'It's OK,' said the Doctor, as Amelia slipped the netting over the wheels. 'I've got you.'

It was the strangest sensation; a sudden drop, and then the strings held taut and they struck a balance, the little plane holding in the great net of the hammock. It bounced along at an angle, Amelia holding on to stay upright.

'Are you sure you want to stay in there?' said the Doctor over the radio. 'I could winch you up here if you like? I've got comfy chairs.'

'I'll stay with my ship thanks,' said Amelia, even as her teeth chattered in her head and she braced herself against the starboard side.

'OK!' said the Doctor. 'Expect a bit of turbulence. But I think I can get you to Howland Island. They're waiting for you there, right?'

'Yup.'

'OK, then.'

'I'll have to ... I'll have to contact Noonan's family.'

'I know,' said the Doctor, and there was silence.

*

Ahead, the day had fully dawned. The sea was as flat as a millpond, the strange outlined shadows of the two ships racing beneath them, never catching up.

Amelia stared over the top of the instrument panel. 'What's that?'

She was looking straight ahead; the Doctor was looking back at her.

'What?'

'Ahead! Why don't you have proper windows on that thing?'

'Well, strictly speaking—'

'*Ahead!*'

The Doctor leant out, at an entirely unsafe angle, and gasped.

Straight ahead of them, cutting a swathe across the bright blue sky was another long vertical line of purple.

'It's not ...?'

'It is,' said the Doctor grimly. 'Amelia. You have to come over here.'

Amelia looked at her plane. 'Can't we fly round them?'

'If they reach the ground – or you, or anyone, any fish, any creature in the ocean – then they'll be here.'

'I'll stay in my plane.'

'You can't – you saw what happened to Noonan.'

Amelia swallowed. 'Well, why will being in your airplane be any better?'

'It just is.' He shook the hammock. 'Hurry up! I mean it.'

'What are you going to do?'

'Seal the hole,' said the Doctor.

'And the ones that have already made it through?'

The Doctor rubbed the back of his neck. 'One thing at a time! Just move, will you?'

The Electra was starting to stutter and stop. It was done. Amelia looked back at the control panel sadly and patted it. Then, resolute, she started to climb the hammock rope, a hundred feet up in the air. The wind whistled around as she balanced, precariously, pulling herself hand over hand as the Doctor slowed the TARDIS to the same speed as Electra, so she was effectively climbing a ladder.

'Come on, Earhart,' he yelled, watching her with admiration. She was absolutely fearless.

Then his face looked to the side and he frowned.

'What is it?' said Amelia, concentrating on where she was putting her feet in the netting.

'Nothing! Don't stop.' He put his hands over his eyes to see better over the sun, now rising in the sky.

'What *is* it?'

The swarm was building in volume now. They had sensed the movement, the possibility of flesh. They were changing direction.

The Doctor stretched his hand down towards her. 'Can you move a little faster?'

Amelia climbed quicker, looking over at the buzzing swarm now heading straight towards them. 'They're coming!'

'Then move! *Move!*'

Amelia scrambled up the last few inches, grabbed his arm and was just about to jump on board when she felt it. Just the tiniest dot, down, in the gap exposed between her flying suit and her boots. The tiniest of stings.

'Come on! Get on board! *Come on!*'

She glanced upwards. 'No,' she said. 'No. I'll be fine. I'll distract them.'

'Get on board!' said the Doctor.

But Amelia had already let go of his hand.

'Could you have handled a swarm in the TARDIS?' said Yaz, looking around.

The Doctor scowled. 'I'd have figured something out.'

Amelia glanced up. She could feel an itching: a crawling feeling, underneath her skin. She knew exactly what it was. She knew exactly what was going to happen. She shook her head.

'No,' she said and began climbing back down. 'No. Let them all come to me.'

'Come here!' shouted the Doctor. 'I need to fix this!'

Amelia shook her head once more.

'*Gaaah!*' shouted the Doctor, glancing at the swarm. They were still coming through. 'Oh, for goodness' sake.'

He listened for the sound of the Electra. It was still running, on fumes, puttering ahead, just about.

'Well, stay in there, then!' he said as Amelia reached back into the cockpit. '*Stay there!* I'm going to seal the hole! I'll be *right back*! Keep gliding until I get back, then I can fix this and I can fix you, do you hear me?'

He shouted into the radio until it squealed with feedback.

'I will be right back!'

Then he jettisoned the hammock, which tumbled on top of the tiny plane, and the TARDIS shot off, directly upwards, following the line to the tiny pinhole in the ozone layer just above the South Pacific.

He grumbled to himself, closing it with careful stitches, in the full and certain knowledge that humans were only going to open it again; but the scuttling fluttering tiny line of creatures stopped.

And then they disappeared.

The Doctor blinked: what had he missed? Where had they gone? He shot the TARDIS back down like a speeding elevator, the colours lightening through every different shade of blue imaginable.

But there was nothing. Nothing where he had been just a moment before. Nothing in the air; nothing on the sea. He checked and rechecked where he'd been. The TARDIS skimmed elegantly, across the very surface of the sea. There wasn't a trace to be seen anywhere. Nor was there any hint of Amelia – no scrap of metal, no piece of fuselage; not a single glove, not a slick of oil.

'Where did she ... What did she do?'

The Doctor shrugged. 'She had her lighter,' she said. 'And there was enough spilt fuel around ... to shoot through the Losiruz like a chain reaction, blow them all to smithereens.'

'Then surely you'd have seen smoke or ...'

'Well, quite,' said the Doctor.

'Are you sure you were in the right spot?'

'I looked. I waited. They'd gone.'

'She blew herself up?'

'I could have ... I could have saved her. But she didn't trust me.'

There was a silence.

'So you definitely don't know where she is?' said Yaz.

The Doctor blinked rapidly. 'You mean, did I finally pick her up, floating on the water, terribly burned from the explosion, clean her up, tend her wounds and then the two of us flew around the galaxy for fifty years, free to explore, without worrying about pursuit from newspapermen, from autograph hunters, from sponsors and disapproving family members? Did I eventually gain her trust and respect her enough for us to be true partners? Did she leave behind her Earth-bound life to be remembered as the glorious ultimate symbol of a free spirit and the bravery and power of womanhood that inspired countless millions?'

There was a long pause.

'Absolutely not. Anyway, shall we get back?'

'Feeling better?' asked the Doctor as they headed back to the control room.

'Yeah,' said Yaz. 'Yeah I am, thanks.'

They headed back up the spiral stairs, along and up the twisting staircase. The Doctor paused, just once, before they got to the fish tank, to open a seemingly random cupboard.

'Just checking,' she said as Yaz peered over her shoulder at the twenty-four large brand new gleaming canisters of gasoline. 'Just in case,' she added.

And she gently shut the cupboard door, and on they went.

That's All Right, Mama

Paul Magrs

The boy was trying hard not to cry. The other kids had got him into the corner of the schoolyard and they were jeering at him, like they always did. He was covered in dirt from scuffling with some of the boys, and there were smudges of tears on his face.

Their teacher hadn't made things any easier for him today. 'That's not what I'd call music,' she'd said, when she got him up at the front of the class and he'd sung for them.

Now in the schoolyard he had his battered toy guitar slung around his neck and he was staring back at them all defiantly, like he always did. They pushed and jostled and laughed at him. Who did he think he was?

He started to play. He strummed the few chords he knew, as hard as he could. And he started to sing again. Loudly, and with all his heart and soul. Just to block them out. Just so he couldn't hear them laughing any more. It was some country song he'd heard on the local radio. He was trying to figure out his own way to sing it. They laughed even more and said he was a hillbilly.

When they eventually left him alone it was only because his mama had appeared in the schoolyard. She was wearing her housecoat out of doors, brightly coloured and floral. Her hair was awry, which was unusual, too.

'Honey,' his mother said. 'We gotta go.'

Who was he to argue? He was glad to get out of school early. He took her hand and off they went.

It wasn't far to their little house. Puzzling thing was, all their belongings seemed to have been dumped outside on the street. They were heaped any old how on the scrubby grass.

'We're leavin' today,' his mama said. 'We gotta move across town to stay with your daddy's sister and her man. You understand, don't you?'

The boy nodded, staring at all their things lying out in the street. He wasn't really sure what was happening at all. Daddy was in jail, he knew that much. He'd gone away just a couple of days ago. Not for nothing really bad. Just something to do with a bad check, that was all; the really criminal thing, Mama said, was that he had to go away as a result of it. There were worse people out there than Daddy, but she guessed that was the law. Mama and the boy would just have to struggle on by themselves for a little while.

But now they were losing the house.

'It's all right, Mama,' he said, squeezing her hand. 'So long as we're still together, nothing else matters.'

Mama looked like she was about to burst into tears at that.

Then a skinny man in a long coat, suit and sneakers came running along the street like he was being chased by something awful. He jumped the fence and held his finger to his lip to keep them quiet. The boy looked at his mama.

'What do you think you're doing?' she asked the stranger. 'You in trouble?'

'Usually. You haven't seen anyone covered in green fur with sort of crystalline extrusions coming out of their foreheads, have you?' The man mimed lumpy bodies while looking worriedly along the street. This guy had amazing hair, standing up on end just about, and great sideburns. Was that what they were called?

'These creatures,' the stranger went on, 'they were messing around with technology they really, really shouldn't have had.' He pulled out two grey boxes from his coat pocket. 'Turns out they'd nicked some super-secret souped-up communicators from a Drahvin tech camp on the outer rim of Galaxy Four.'

'Communicators?' said Mama.

'Yeah, like telephones. Telephones that work in space and do all sorts of other stuff. Weird who-knows-what stuff! Some of those Drahvin boffins, oh, they're smart. Smart as paint! Sentient paint, with an IQ of—'

'What the hell are you talking about?'

'So, anyway, I stepped in pretty sharpish and confiscated the communicators and ooh, look! What a lovely gramophone player!'

Mama was carrying the record player as if it was the most precious thing that the family owned. Which it was, the boy realised. It was fancy and expensive but it was also his favourite thing. He had been in awe of that machine and the music that came out of it for as long as he could remember.

Mama frowned at the stranger and looked him up and down. 'Look, Mister ...'

'Doctor.'

'Doctor. Look, I haven't been following a word you been saying to me, but would you carry these suitcases for me to our new home? It's only about twelve blocks south.'

'Like a removals man! Good cover. Blend in. Clever!'

'I'd be much obliged, sir.'

The Doctor beamed at her. 'It would be a pleasure! And all the rest of this stuff?' He surveyed their belongings, which all looked a bit worn and like poor people's stuff lying there in the yard. 'Do you want it all carrying over to the new place?'

She smiled ruefully. 'If it'll all fit. It's only a room at the back of my sister-in-law's place we're goin' to, but beggars can't be choosers.'

'I know what you mean.' The Doctor dropped his little grey boxes into an old carpet bag, and started chatting away again. 'Anyway, turns out these green furry fellas have programmed a pair of drone assassins to pinch back the comms tech and obliterate me. So, here's the thing, if I could maybe just leave the communicators with you for a bit? Just while I lead the assassins off-world so they can't hurt anyone here ...'

The boy was listening more attentively than his mother, carrying a box load of records with his toy guitar balanced on top. 'You mean like outer space men?' he asked the stranger suddenly. 'Is that who you're talking about?'

The man with the gigantic quiff in his hair looked delighted. 'Yes! Yes! That's exactly what I'm talking about!'

But Mama was getting impatient now. 'Come on, you guys. We gotta get all this stuff moved tonight. Stop dawdling, now!'

'Yeah. Right. Course.' The man looked pained. 'But if you could just—'

'No wasting time chatting about outer space nonsense!' Mama ambled ahead, up the sidewalk, through the slanting rays of the evening sun. It was late autumn and still warm. The air was like molasses and everything was slow, apart from this bustling, capable woman, trying to maintain her dignity as she carried that old record player to her relatives' house. 'Come on, now.'

'All right, Mama,' shrugged the boy.

'Good boy, Elvis,' she smiled.

'Come on, Doctor,' the boy said.

The Doctor almost dropped the carpet bag and stared at him. 'Elvis? Did she just call you *Elvis*?'

It was years later. Mama and Daddy had a new house, in a slightly better part of town. Elvis was almost fully grown, and he was dressing like no one else in school. He combed back his dark hair with oil and wore tapered black pants with a pink stripe down them. No one walked about with a swagger like he did.

But when he swaggered into Sun Records that day he was nervous.

He had saved the four dollars he needed to hire the studio and record his song. He had taken ages, choosing which song to sing for his mama on her birthday. He still couldn't believe that all he had to do was turn up with the money, and his guitar, sing his number and then they'd give him a real vinyl recording to play at home. It seemed like magic, or something from outer space.

When he built up the nerve to go inside the building he found a perfectly ordinary office. There was a desk with a normal-looking middle-aged secretary sitting there. She was neat and smiling, and asking him what he wanted.

Elvis managed to stammer out what it was he was after. He kept looking at the floor and his legs were trembling, as they always did when he was nervous.

'What kind of singing is it you do?' the lady asked. 'Who are you like?'

He shrugged. 'I ain't like anyone, ma'am.'

As he said this, Elvis was aware of another young man, who was sitting in the waiting room and reading the funny papers. 'Ha!' he burst out. 'How true! How true!' When the man lowered the colourful pages, Elvis saw a bow tie and the most extravagant pompadour he'd ever seen a young man wear. How did he manage to get his hair like that? 'Just you be yourself!' the young stranger urged him. 'You'll show them! Haha!'

Elvis had no idea who the young guy was, but he was talking like they were familiar somehow. Had they been at school together maybe? Elvis wasn't sure, but he couldn't remember ever meeting anyone with an English accent before. This guy sounded like someone from a war movie.

'Elvis ...?' asked the secretary, standing up and gesturing with her clipboard for him to follow her. 'If you'd like to come through to the studio now ...?'

His heart was thrumming like he had steel guitar strings inside of himself.

'Just before you make your first ever record – and history! – it's history I've been wanting to talk to you about.' The young stranger grinned at him, also standing up. 'I've left it a little while, I'm afraid, there's always something needs doing. But do you remember a skinny man in a striped suit who left some funny telephones in little grey boxes round your house ...?'

Elvis frowned. He'd not thought of that day in years. 'The Doctor?'

'The Doctor!' The young man straightened his bow tie with a bashful grin. 'You see, the Doctor has sent me to collect those grey boxes ...'

But then the nice secretary lady was taking Elvis by the arm and dragging him into the recording studio. Elvis glanced at the stranger. 'I have no idea. But I bet Mama knows.'

'I'll ask her!' The Doctor nodded. 'Splendid idea. Excellent. That's what I'll do!'

In the meantime, Elvis had to go and record his first song – for his mama's birthday – and all thoughts of that crazy stranger in the waiting room evaporated. Once Elvis emerged to wait for his recording to be pressed and to hold that actual disc in his hands, the stranger was gone.

*

Three years later, everything had changed forever.

Elvis was driving around in a Pink Cadillac. He was off somewhere in Arizona. If only his mama could see him, he thought. Speeding through the desert in his brand new car. Every cent of it paid for. Every cent of it earned in just a few months.

He was on his way to being a star. He knew it. He'd always known it. Deep in his heart. He'd been nervous once or twice, sure, but he'd been brave and did what he knew how to do. He sang with all his heart and soul and did it the best he could. He always knew that people were going to listen to him in the end. And now they really were. Look! He had the car of his dreams already, and he was only twenty.

He wished his mama could see this. But he'd soon be home. He'd bring this home to show her. See, Mama? The Colonel was right. All of this can be mine. Ours. He's the right manager for me. He was right about that. It just means being away from home for longer periods. That's all. You'll understand, Mama. If I can make enough money, I can buy you a big house. When I have enough money I can stay home forever. We'll be together in comfort, and never worry again.

He put his foot down on the pedal and roared through the broiling canyons, with many, many hours still to go before he was anywhere near home.

In Memphis, Gladys was fretting. She paced her living room, muttering to herself. She wept and moaned and tried to calm down. She just had a bad feeling about this new car business. She hated the fact that she didn't know what he was up to. Out on the road, at his age. That Colonel Tom Parker and all his promises! It was pie in the sky. There was something about it all she didn't like or trust. Her son was a good boy. He would always be a good boy if he listened to his conscience and remembered what his mama had told him.

But still Gladys fretted and paced around wearing out the good new rug in her living room. If only she could be sure he was all right … Why didn't he call?

She was interrupted in her worrying by a knock at the front door. 'Yes …?'

'Mrs Presley?' The gangly tall guy grinned at her. He was all in black, with a shock of white hair and black sunglasses. He looked like a grinning funeral director, except he was slightly unkempt. His tailcoat was dusty and singed in places and his shirt cuffs hung down raggedly.

'I don't need anything today,' she smiled, starting to close the door. He was obviously a crazy salesperson. 'I already got a vacuum cleaner.'

'It's actually you who have something *I* need, Mrs Presley.' He peered at her. 'Two little grey boxes to be precise. I've been meaning to call round for some time. They were left with you for safekeeping by a man in a pinstripe suit …'

Gladys stiffened. 'I wouldn't know anything about those.'

'Oh?' The man's smile seemed to be causing him a certain amount of suffering. 'Only, I took some readings …'

'I don't care what you've been reading. That was years ago. We've moved three times since then. That ratty old carpet bag and anything inside it must be long gone.'

'Much like the assassin drones I lured into that supernova. Lost ...'

A bright, chiming noise from the closet jarred the awkward silence.

Gladys tried to shut the door. 'I have to go.'

The man planted his foot in the door, his face grave. 'Not, perhaps, as lost as you thought?'

'Mama?' Elvis's voice burst from the closet. 'You around? You gonna pick up?'

The undertaker's eyes were searching out hers. 'You've kept this your secret? Nobody knows? Only, if those boxes were to fall into the wrong hands ...'

'Nobody.' Gladys felt terror at the thought of the precious gift of being able to contact her boy any time and place being taken away from her. 'Please, sir, you must know the man in the pinstripes who blessed us with them? Well, he said the boxes were secret and, me and Elvis, we'd never betray that secret. Neither of us would. You've got to believe me.'

'Mama?' Elvis's voice again.

'Every noise he makes is from the heart, isn't it?' The undertaker smiled, a real, genuine smile this time, at the sound of her son. 'You know, I'm a big fan, whichever ears I'm wearing. I tell you what. Blind eye being turned, for now. Just for now. Not a word though, eh?' And then, in a swirl of coat tails, the stranger was gone. 'Until next time, Mrs Presley!'

As soon as the door was closed, Gladys crossed to the closet and took the tiny machine and pressed the button. 'Elvis ...? Where are you, honey ...?'

'I'm in Arizona, Mama,' her boy was telling her. For the hundredth time she marvelled at how clear his voice was. Once they'd figured out how the boxes let you talk across the air, they'd agreed only to use them in emergencies, in case the green furry fellas with the crystal horns ever came looking.

'Mama, don't go crazy but I had a little accident ...'

'An accident!' she gasped.

'The car caught fire ...' he mumbled sheepishly. 'Yeah, my brand new pink Cadillac. The engine burst into flames. I'm sitting by the roadside here, waiting for the repair truck ... I'm gonna be late. But I reckon the car will be just fine.'

Gladys felt sad. It seemed like her boy was always gonna be so far away. His life and all his new success – it was going to take him far away from her all the time now, wasn't it?

'I'd better go. The tow-truck is here. I love you, Mama.' There was a beep, and then he was gone.

Elvis stayed indoors that day and cried and cried.

Mama was gone forever, and he hadn't been there at the end. Too busy on the road. Too busy working and getting lost in his music. She had begged him to come home, to stop working, and he just hadn't listened. Now she was gone forever.

He stayed on his bed in the army barracks. The grey box rested on his chest. He'd give anything for that old connection back. Just the thought of pressing that green button once more …

Say, he didn't even know where Mama's phone was. After she died, where had it vanished to?

He pressed the green button.

There was ringing at the other end. Clicking.

'Hello …?'

It was *her*.

It couldn't be, but it was.

It was impossible but somehow it was true.

'M-Mama …?'

'Hey, son. It's lovely to hear your voice.' She sounded so casual. So ordinary. She didn't sound like someone who'd died.

He sat up on the bed and his heart was racing. He was going crazy. The stress of the work was getting to him. He was going out of his mind …

'Elvis …?' she asked. 'Are you OK …?'

'Mama … what day is it?'

She laughed. 'Land sakes' boy, but you're losing your grip on the real world if you don't remember the day … !'

'It's serious, Mama! What date is it?'

A pause, and then she told him the day that it was at her end of the phone.

It was the very date that she had died. A month ago.

'W-what time is it, Mama …?'

'Why, it's early afternoon here, son. Which State are you in today? Your mind's all in a whirl with the time difference, ain't it?'

The time difference. Yes. It had certainly put him in a whirl. 'But Mama, you're talking just naturally, just normally … like you ain't even …'

She broke in to his stammering flow of words: 'Ain't even what, son …?'

Now he couldn't say it. He could hardly tell her that she was supposed to be dead. He mumbled some excuses to cover himself, saying he'd only just woken up. His head was all in a muddle.

'You get yourself some proper sleep,' she warned him. 'I don't like hearing you sounding so confused!'

He talked to her like it was all the most natural thing in the world, and in some ways it was. But as their call ended that afternoon he was left staring at that strange grey box and thinking: *I was just talking to my mama on the very day of her death.*

That special connection. Somehow it's still there between us.

It was much later, and a different lifetime altogether. The Doctor and her three friends were aboard the TARDIS following their terrifying adventure with giant spiders in a luxury hotel in Sheffield.

'I do not!' she protested, laughing, just minutes after the four of them had pulled the dematerialisation switch together, sending the ship spinning into the time-space vortex.

'But you do!' Yasmin told her. 'You namedrop all the time. We never know whether half the stuff you say is true.'

'She's right, Doc,' Graham chuckled. 'All these historical celebrities you reckon you've met. They can't all be for real. There just isn't time for you to have met them all!'

The Doctor gave him a funny look. 'There's all the time in the world aboard the TARDIS.'

A thought occurred to Ryan, as he stood there watching the dizzying lights of the console and the crystalline machinery as it rose and fell. 'What about Elvis Presley, then? You said you gave him a mobile phone. Was that just a joke?'

For a second the Doctor looked perturbed. 'How else did we get hold of Sinatra in the 50s, eh? Knew he'd lend it out to 'Ol Blue Eyes. Genius move by me. Not at all dodgy.'

Her three friends were looking at her as she busied herself at the console. 'Why did you give him a mobile phone?' asked Graham.

'I didn't! It was some experimental tech I pinched from some very notorious interstellar tech-thieves and hid round his place when he was small. Him and his mum worked out how to use them, though, and …' The Doctor wrinkled her nose. 'He could phone his mum when he was on the road touring, and she could phone him. She was very worried about him because he was so young and he'd never been away from home, and I felt sorry for her.'

'Oh, bless!' Yaz said. 'I think that's lovely.'

'It's kind of bending the laws of time a little,' the Doctor admitted.

'Well,' said Graham. 'It didn't do any harm, did it?'

'Funny you should say that,' said the Doctor darkly. 'Since I got the TARDIS back, and while I was waiting for you lot, she's been sweating a bit. Like something's not quite right with the web of time.'

'Do NOT mention webs.' Ryan shuddered.

'Calling that phone like we did, the TARDIS tapped into its transmissions … and she is not happy. Things might be a little bit awry. I might have caused all kinds of damage to the timelines. I could be a bit daft and reckless in my earlier lives, you know?'

'Anyway,' Ryan shrugged. 'It never did Elvis any harm. He's still doing pretty well. How old's he now? Eighty-two or something?'

The Doctor froze. 'Hang on. What did you say? Elvis is still *alive*?'

'Of course!' Ryan said. 'He's never left the house in years. Graceland, is that where he lives? He's retired and that. But he's still alive. We'd have heard about it if the King of Rock and Roll had died, wouldn't we?'

'He did! August 1977! The whole world's supposed to know about it!' The Doctor started leaping and dashing around the console, turning dials and jabbing at buttons. 'Oh no no no no no no! It can't be true …! It just can't …!'

But it was. Elvis Aaron Presley was still alive and well in the year 2018. His luxurious estate Graceland had become a kind of fortress, and the King carried on living a secluded life, away from the world's media and any other prying eyes. Only the very trusted inner circle of employees got to visit the deepest recesses of Graceland, where Elvis dwelled, looking fit and healthy and slim in his trademark jumpsuits in various pastel shades.

He ate vegan burgers and drank vegetable smoothies. He was the healthiest 82-year-old on the planet.

He spent most of his time reliving past glories: watching his old movies and recordings of his concerts played back on a wall of television screens in his bedroom. Sometimes he toyed with the idea of making a comeback. Surprising the whole world. He was the world's very first rock and roll star. Who was to say he couldn't come blazing back with a new album even at this advanced age?

Mostly, though, he preferred to sit at home and eat healthy food and think back over past glories, and remember all the people he had loved and lost.

Really, he felt pretty lonely.

Even talking on the phone to his mama didn't help. Hearing her voice echoing through that little old device of his: it just sounded so far away in both time and space. He was eking out the few minutes they had left. He knew that this magical connection between them couldn't last forever. The display on the phone was growing slightly fainter – he knew it – day by day. It was a miracle, really, that it had lasted this long.

So his thoughts were running along these lines – almost psychically – on the morning that the TARDIS materialised within the hallowed, ultra-high security fences of Graceland. Upstairs, watching his 1968 TV special for the millionth time, Elvis was vaguely aware of an unfamiliar *vworping* noise coming from outside. His staff would sort that out, whatever it was. He didn't feel like getting up to investigate. For some reason, he was feeling blue and dissatisfied today. Even his brunch wasn't up to scratch. Perhaps what he really fancied was a real, juicy, proper hamburger made of meat? And a really sugary milkshake? Or a fried bacon, peanut butter and banana sandwich? Oh, but these were bad thoughts from the dark times. His mama had taught him to eat better than that.

There was some noise just then, from the corridor outside his vast bedroom. His bodyguards were yelling. Something was wrong. There were intruders!

The bedroom door flew open and four very unusual figures came striding across his fluffy white carpet. Three of the figures were perfectly ordinary looking. They were like tourists, eyes all agog at seeing the King's luxurious inner sanctum. They were led by a determined-looking blonde woman with high cheekbones and what looked like clown's pants held up by suspenders and also a long blue coat that flared out behind her. She looked like she meant business as she marched fearlessly up to the King of Graceland.

'Elvis!' she grinned, and her face lit up at the sight of him. 'Oh, you would never recognise me. But you met… ah, my colleagues in the past. Some of them. I'm the Doctor, and this is Yaz, Graham and Ryan. We're all huge fans.'

'Amazing,' Ryan said.

Graham just beamed at him. Yaz was looking nervously behind them, worrying about the security guards that the Doctor had knocked out with that weird Venusian aikido of hers.

'I don't know how to say this, Elvis,' said the Doctor, 'but you're living on borrowed time. Well, *pinched* time, really. This can't go on.'

'Huh?' he said tetchily. This young woman was making no sense.

'Give me the phone,' she said. 'I know you've still got it.'

'The phone?' he gasped, holding it tightly in his hand and pressing it to his chest.

'You know!' she said insistently. 'The souped-up Drahvin communicator devices!'

Elvis's mouth fell open in astonishment.

'I hate to tell you this, but those walkie-talkies are causing all kinds of wobbles in the web of time. The wrong singles are getting to the top of the Billboard charts, and there's a war broken out in a country that shouldn't even exist. See? Big and small stuff radiating out through the … erm … damage that's already been caused …' The Doctor was gabbling and looking worried. 'Nothing is exactly apocalyptic. Well, not yet. But nevertheless, I've got to sort it out. And you're going to help me. Show me the phone.'

He looked so old! The Doctor could hardly believe it. In the true timeline, Elvis had become overweight and had died when he was still relatively young. This Elvis was lean and weathered like a piece of old driftwood. His quiffed hair was stark white. Slowly, he opened his palm to reveal the communicator.

'There it is.' She waved his protests away. 'You've got to come with us, Elvis.'

Graham let out a squeak of excitement. 'We're taking Elvis with us?'

The Doctor nodded and offered Elvis a hand up from his Pilates ball. 'Into time and space, yep. It's the only way.'

Elvis stared at them. 'But I can't leave Graceland! I haven't been in the world out there for years . . .!'

The Doctor took his hand. 'Then maybe it's time you did . . .?'

Graham watched Yaz and Ryan as they looked after their guest as best they could: finding somewhere comfortable for him to sit, and watching as he coped with the amazing sight of the ship's impossible interior. If only Grace were here! She would be amazed at how blasé those two kids were being about meeting the King. 'You can see that he's like ... iconic, can't you?' Graham said, almost to himself. 'There's like a kind of shimmering light about him ...' He frowned and stared harder. There was definitely a glimmering light playing around the old man's jumpsuit.

'That's not stardust. That's part of the problem ...' The Doctor frowned worriedly. 'I told you, Elvis was supposed to die in 1977.'

'But he's always taken such care of himself!'

'It wasn't always like that. And now that we've taken him out of your timeline . . .' She was flipping switches and studying readings. 'Everything's started to go a bit wonky.'

'Wonky?' Graham asked.

'I'm not sure how long we've got,' she said, biting her lip.

It took some persuading, but eventually Elvis surrendered his precious mobile phone to the Doctor. He was drinking a glass of water in an alcove with Ryan and Yaz, and telling them tales of his past glories. 'You will … uh, give me it back, won't you?'

The Doctor promised she would. The device looked ancient now. The symbols on its buttons were almost worn smooth by time and use.

She took it with due reverence over to the console and placed it carefully on the sensors of the telepathic circuits. Then she stretched out her arm and trained the sonic on it. There was a shower of sparks and a babble of human voices, suddenly filling the air of the TARDIS. Everyone jumped, and she hurriedly turned down the volume. 'Sorry …!'

A wispy, blue pattern of light appeared above the console: a kind of three-dimensional call history emanating from the futuristic phone. The Doctor's eyebrows went up. The device was absolutely covered in traces of Artron energy, just as she suspected.

'Erm, Elvis,' she said, calling him over. 'Are you still calling your mum up on this phone?'

He grinned and loped over, and then looked alarmed when he saw all that crazy blue light coming out of his phone. But something – he wasn't sure what – made him trust this Doctor. 'Why, yes, ma'am,' he answered. 'Of course I do. Even at my age.'

'Eighty-two!' Graham said. 'How old does that make your mum, then?'

Elvis looked away. 'Why, the same age as ever.'

Yaz and Ryan had rejoined them at the console, looking just as confused as Graham.

The Doctor put things very simply for them: 'Elvis, tell them the truth. That your mother passed away from kidney failure and heart disease in 1958, while you were in the army.'

Elvis's face went dark and haunted-looking. Like he had no idea what to say.

'But how?' Ryan asked bluntly. 'How's he been able to carry on talking to her?'

Gladys Presley spent her last day on Earth in her dressing gown and nightie. She kept her rollers in for most of the day. Maybe this afternoon she'd set her hair nicely. Maybe doll herself up a little. Just on the off-chance her boy would turn up. She'd want to be looking her best for him.

She was a practical woman. She wasn't a sentimental fool. She knew she didn't have long left in this world. She felt weary, and it took all her energy just moving from room to room round the house her son had bought for her. Each day saw her winding down a little more, like a clockwork toy, and today really felt like the worst yet.

But there was something special about today. It was her red letter day. It felt, really, more like a birthday than a death day.

Somehow, maybe magically, she was getting a lot of attention today. Her phone just never stopped ringing. Every few minutes, it seemed like. That funny little phone – so small, it was kind of like a child's toy – it would ring shrilly and she'd hurry over to her comfy chair and bleep it open.

'Elvis . . .?'

Her voice was hopeful and girlish-sounding. She marvelled that she could sound so happy and pain-free.

It was important to her not to give away how rotten she felt, what with him being so far away.

That last day went by, hour by hour. A warm, sunny day with the windows open and the curtains rustling. Coffee percolating on the stove. Her boy talking to her on the phone.

First, in the morning, he was bright and cheery and excited. He was here, there and everywhere. Playing concerts in different towns and states. Travelling everywhere with the Colonel. Swanking about in his vast pink car. He laughed so much when he talked about the way the girls screamed at his antics. How he shook his legs when he sang and it only started out because he was so scared. Oh, but they screamed at the sight of him and loved the way he moved, so he had to keep it in the act...

He didn't just tell her about his successes. He asked for her advice, too. These films his manager wanted him to star in. Should he go all the way to Hollywood and live there for months? If he was going to act, he wanted to do it properly. If he was really going to be a star, he was going to throw his whole self into it...

And that meant being away from home even more. Even longer stretches of time. Years and years...

And the army. Selective Service. It would look good to the public if he went and served his time. He shaved his head. They filmed him having all his hair shaved off at the barbers. He went to Germany and said he wanted to be treated like all the rest.

But he wasn't like all the rest. He was her Elvis, and he was too far away from her. Especially now, on what felt to Gladys like the last day of her life.

She had a very strong feeling, about lunchtime on that day, as she fixed herself a sandwich in that brand new kitchen of hers: she had a dreadful feeling that she was never going to see that boy of hers again. Not in the actual flesh. Time was running out …

But then, that afternoon in 1958, the phone calls simply carried on coming. The first one after lunch came from a date in 1958 she had never lived to see. And soon both mother and son realised that something miraculous was occurring.

The crowd was vast and noisy. The whole stadium was shaking with their cheering and stamping, so much that no one noticed the battered blue Police Box materialising in one of the concrete stairwells.

'Are we at a footie match?' Ryan asked as Team TARDIS emerged with elderly Elvis in tow.

'Hmm,' the Doctor thought. 'Our geriatric rock star is really starting to glimmer and glow around the edges by now. I wonder how much time we've got left?'

Graham was grinning. 'It's not the footie, Ryan. That's not a football chant they're singing out there …'

'It's "Suspicious Minds",' Yaz said. 'My nani loves that song. She said it was like her and my granddad's whole story but she's never explained why …'

'We must be at Wembley Stadium …' Elvis said quietly. '1983. The biggest show I ever played, even bigger than Michigan …' He looked even more ashen than seconds before as he turned to the Doctor. 'But ma'am … how can that be? Can you really carry us back in time?'

The Doctor shrugged happily. 'Backwards, forwards, diagonally … just about anywhere, really. Even into hypothetical realities and dimensions where things have gone slightly wrong …'

But Elvis had already turned away, and was tottering off up the stairwell that led into the stadium.

'Better get after him!' the Doctor urged. 'We don't want to lose him here in 1983 … And we'd best get him before anyone notices him …'

'How come he's glowing round the edges?' Ryan threw back the question as he dashed up the steps.

'Sequins,' the Doctor said. 'He had them sewn into everything.'

Yaz gave her a funny look, discerning the Time Lord's real mood under her flippancy. 'You're really worried about this.'

'I keep saying, he really shouldn't be here, Yaz. Time is out of joint, and it's all my fault, and that glowing isn't just sequins … it's a kind of danger sign …'

Graham patted her on the shoulder. 'Then we'd better get after him'

They found him standing on the terraces, in the thick of the crowd, and mercifully no one was taking very much notice. They were all staring at the pulsating lightshow at the other end of the stadium, and the gigantic screens that showed an Elvis in his middle years, giving it his all in a high-collared jumpsuit not unlike the one his older self was wearing.

'I … was *fantastic* … !' the old man said, barely audible under the screaming of the crowd. He stood there in raptures, mouthing along with the words. The Doctor was just glad no one had noticed him there but, as she glanced around the crowd, she noticed quite a few fans in Elvis cosplay. Of course no one would pay any attention to yet another, particularly a wizened old man.

'Thank you, Doctor,' he said, turning to her.

She didn't look at him, eyes closed like she was concentrating on something hard to catch, beyond the music. 'I've been hoping there was one certain event that triggered the worst of the divergence. One thing that we could avoid so …'

'So?'

'So I wouldn't have to take all this away. From you, from everyone.' She looked at him, so sad. 'A world with Elvis in it is a better world. But it's too much, the ripples of your being here have put too much out of true.'

'I don't understand what you're saying,' said Elvis. 'I'm not meant to be here?'

'We have to keep moving backwards,' the Doctor said. 'I just need to find the point at which this time stream deviates from the real one … Maybe we should try ten years ago in Las Vegas … see what we can do there to protect the real time stream …'

'What do you mean, the "real time stream"?' Elvis gestured around at that heaving stadium, and all the singing, joyous people. Eighty thousand people singing along with him. 'Isn't this real?'

She shook her head sadly. 'This is England, Elvis. You never toured here. You never toured the world.'

'But I did!' he burst out, looking almost feverish as he yelled out over the noise his other self was making. 'We toured Japan and Australia and all of Europe. We were on tour for the whole of the 1980s and 1990s! Are you saying that I imagined all of that …?' He laughed at her, shaking his head.

'Yes! No! I mean …' She couldn't get it through to him. How could she tell him that he never toured because Colonel Tom Parker wouldn't let him go further than Hawaii? That he spent his later years in Las Vegas, never leaving his glitzy hotel, playing shows night after night, dreaming of travelling the world? There was no kind way of telling him all of that … or that he never actually lived past 1977.

'Come on, Elv,' she said. 'We'd best get back to the TARDIS.'

Ryan had reappeared from the burger van with snacks for everyone. 'Sorry, I only eat macrobiotic food,' Elvis told him politely.

Back in the TARDIS, the Doctor was studying the vaporous trails of light that were emanating from Elvis's mobile phone and the console. She nodded as she followed the patterns, and shook her head as she realised what they meant.

'Tell me again what we're looking at here,' Elvis said. His keenness to understand and to learn touched the Doctor's hearts. Most other people would be frustrated and angry at being dragged from their home and being confronted by things that seemed impossible. Not Elvis. 'Oh, I read books,' he told her. 'I got turned on to philosophy and metaphysics and the mysteries of life in the 1960s by my hairdresser. I find all this stuff fascinating. And I believe that there is something bigger than us, guiding us, and making sure we do things in a certain way … I believe we have to listen to their messages and their guidance …'

'Well,' said the Doctor, 'I'll tell you what I know. These lines in the air here … they are the timelines. Here's your progress through history, mapped into five dimensions, see? And this is the life of your mother, Gladys Presley.'

'It seems so little, compared …'

'And here are the calls you made using this phone that I … erm, my colleagues gave you when you were young. See how the calls are spread evenly along your timeline, but their recipient gets them all in one afternoon? Back in 1958?'

'Time has stood still for Mama,' he nodded. 'That's what I always figured. Somehow … magically … she was caught forever in that golden afternoon, of that final day.'

Graham stared at him. 'You thought it was something magical?'

'Yes, sir,' said Elvis. 'I thought it was God, or the universe, or something. Allowing me to carry on talking to Mama, and receiving her best wishes and all her love, throughout my life. I thought it was a special thing only for us, that only I knew about.'

'That's amazing …!' Ryan breathed.

'I think it sounds lovely,' said Yaz. 'But surely you knew it couldn't really have been magic?'

Elvis suddenly looked tearful. 'Why not? Why shouldn't I have believed in magic all my life? I'm just a boy from a wooden shack in Tupelo, Mississippi. Why should I become the one that the whole world listens to?

Isn't there a kind of magic in that? Why shouldn't I end up believing in all kinds of impossible things? How could I even tell what's real?'

'He's got a point,' Graham mused.

Elvis sobbed, and those lights around his silhouette glittered sharply. 'When I got the news she was dying, I raced to be at her side. I left my barracks and dropped everything. I drove as fast as I could. But I never made it in time. I never saw her again, face to face. It broke my heart in two.'

'I'm sorry,' said the Doctor.

'But I learned that I could still talk to her. And she could talk to me.'

'When did you realise that?' the Doctor asked. She knew deep down that it was hopeless to keep flipping back through time, searching for the turning points … They had to go back to the critical moment, the day when time was chipped away by the future hammering at the past. It was the moment that this miracle needed nipping in the bud.

'Germany,' he said. 'About a month after the funeral. The army took me all the way to Germany, and Daddy too. And I was just so lonely. I went out of my head, just about. And … one night … without even thinking about it … I was in my room, a little drunk on German beer. I took out that phone and I pressed the green button. Like it could still work. It rang only three times and then … she answered … !'

They travelled next to 1960 and a certain American military base stuck out in the middle of Germany where it was pouring with rain. They arrived just in time to see a young Elvis Presley singing his heart out for his fellow recruits, on a cobbled-together stage on the parade ground in a lull between downpours. His face was wet when he sang, as he wept for the thought that his mama would never hear him sing again.

'Bit different to being at Wembley Stadium,' Graham said ruefully, as the show finished. However humble the staging, though, Elvis's performance had been magnificent.

It was that night, after the show, when everyone had slapped his back and ruffled his shorn hair, that Elvis sloped off to the furthest corner of the barracks and pressed the green button on his phone. Even though his mama was dead as far as the whole world knew, he was still phoning her, to keep her abreast of his news.

The Doctor and her friends were just a few yards away, listening in on this moment. The older Elvis was there too, shining in the rain like his body was filled with stardust: remembering every single second of this strange episode.

'Elvis ...? Is that you, my boy?'

Sometimes the young man felt like he was losing his mind. It couldn't be her. It was just impossible. And yet, here she was still, each time he pressed that green button: still alive.

'Mama, you're still there ...?'

She calmly, happily, answered his questions. Then he replied to hers. She was amazed to learn he was in Germany. She was astonished to hear that his father was there too. She was glad that he had met the girl of his dreams in Priscilla. And then she was amazed and enchanted to learn that he was speaking to her from the year 1960.

'The future . . . !' she gasped, realising full well that she herself wasn't in it.

The revelation and the gap of time between them set them both off crying again. The distance seemed too cruel. But then she was the one to calm them both. To make it seem better again with coaxing words, the way she always had done. 'Elvis, sweetheart . . . listen . . . we have a wonderful gift here. This is a wonderful thing. Whatever this is . . . this link between us . . . it's a way of cheating the end, don't you see? It's proof, somehow . . . that the link between us will never end . . .'

'I see that,' he said, choking with grief all over again. 'I know that, Mama.'

Eventually they finished the call, and he promised he would ring again soon. 'Don't you forget!' she laughed, and then the line clicked and he was left alone in the foreign rain.

The Doctor and her friends watched the young man walk home to his bed in the little house on the military base.

'I remember how I felt,' old Elvis said, his voice full of wonder. 'I thought it was a miracle, every time we got to talk again.'

The Doctor touched his arm gently. 'You must take the phone off him,' she said. 'You've got to sneak into your own house while he sleeps and retrieve that phone. That's the way to set history right.'

*

They waited outside the house while the older Elvis snuck indoors to complete his mission. He was really glowing now. Flickering blue, like old-fashioned television pictures reflected on the wall.

'He's fading away, isn't he?' said Yaz.

The Doctor nodded ruefully. 'Older, healthier, wiser Elvis is becoming more and more hypothetical as his timeline corrodes and history returns to its proper order.'

Graham sighed. 'Is there no way of saving him, Doc? That old guy's lived to a contented old age. Does he really have to fade away?'

She smiled sadly. 'It happens to everyone, Graham.'

'I know that,' he said. 'Well. It's not all been bad, has it – I mean, for him it's five years since he lent the phone to Frank Sinatra, and if you hadn't gotten hold of him …'

'Elvis said he got Frankie to sing down the phone to his mum to surprise her – she was a big fan.' Ryan laughed. 'That must've blown her mind!'

They waited for Elvis to creep like a lambent blue ghost to his own bedside and spirit the mobile phone away. It took longer than they expected, and it was a worry: maybe he'd decided not to bother. Maybe he wanted to save his own skin. Maybe the younger self had awakened and caught a glimpse of the old man stealing into the room and haunting himself?

'It's crazy,' the Doctor sighed. 'All these years I've faced menaces and villains who want to change history to their own advantage, and who tamper with the web of time. And here's one who's been most effective of all, and it's someone's mum. And all she's done to create vast cosmic ripples is to carry on chatting to her son after her death. She's guided him with love and good advice, and that's changed history. Telling him to lay off the sleeping pills and the prescription drugs and the booze and the hamburgers and all the things that made him ill.'

'I bet she told him to sack that manager of his, the Colonel, too,' Graham said. 'I bet it was her who did that.'

'And when he marries Priscilla, she'd have told him not to let her get away,' the Doctor added. 'Because, you know, in the real universe, he loses her. He neglects her and he loses her. And everything winds up going wrong for him. He makes a brilliant comeback or two, and everyone loves him, but then …'

'Will our memories change?' Yaz asked. 'Will we always think he died forty years ago or …?'

Graham coughed. 'Shush now, he's coming back.'

The lonesome ghost in the one-piece suit was doddering out of the front door. The Doctor dashed to meet him. 'Did you get the phone?'

He held it up almost reluctantly. 'I got it.'

She made as if to take it. 'Please,' she said. 'It's important.'

'But if I give you this, everything in my life will be different, won't it? I'll miss out on all those calls. All that advice my mama gave me from beyond the grave?'

The Doctor nodded. 'I'm afraid so.'

'But you say it's important that I give it back to you? That I forgo that miracle? For the sake of the rest of the world?'

She smiled gently. 'That's right. I meant it. Small things can cause big ripples. The changes that the phones caused in your life will make wars happen. Bombs will fall. People will die. History will go wrong. I mean it, Elvis. It's deadly serious, this business.'

He nodded, looking amazed and shocked. Then he said, 'Then if I do lose my miracle forever, will you grant me one more wish with your magic time machine, Doctor?'

He handed her the phone and took her arm and she felt him pulsating and glowing with light as she led him and the others back to the TARDIS.

Minutes later they were in Graceland, halfway round the world in Memphis, and two years earlier in time.

'Glory be,' Elvis breathed, as they stepped out onto the manicured lawn into purple twilight. 'I'm home again.'

It was the Graceland of his youth: just how it was when he was a young man, soon after buying the home of his dreams.

Beyond the portico and the tall white pillars all the lights were burning a warm apricot and yellow.

'Will you come with me and meet her?' the King asked his new friends.

So they entered the palace together in the hush of early evening and found the whole house in eerie silence.

'There's no sign of Daddy, or the servants or anyone else,' the elderly Elvis observed. 'They say she sent everyone away. She knew it was the end. She knew it was the final day. She was tired from everything. From fighting her sickness, and all the tears. And she was tired, too, from talking all day on the phone. All day she had listened to her boy getting older and older, growing from a boy to a man to a much older man: living a whole lifetime in just one day.'

The Doctor smiled, gazing around at the opulent splendour of the rooms of Elvis's mansion. 'A whole lifetime in just one day. That's a wonder in itself.'

He led the way upstairs to his mama's private room.

Inside it was like a cosy little grotto of warm light. Everything was comfortable and delightful. She had everything she needed.

At least, she had everything she needed now.

'My son,' she said, as soon as the door opened. She recognised him at once. 'You're my son.'

Graham squeezed the Doctor's arm. They hung back in the corridor. 'She knows him, even though he's twice her age.'

The Doctor sighed. 'That's what it's like when time does funny things. Time Lords recognise each other with their hearts. It's the only way. The same seems true of Elvis and Gladys.'

They watched from a respectful distance as Elvis hugged his mama.

Ryan gave a kind of suppressed whimper inside his chest and Yaz put her arm around him.

Elvis lifted up his head and called to them. 'Hey, these are my friends, Mama. They brought me here. Faster than anyone else ever could. They brought me here to see you, just in time.'

Gladys welcomed them all in and fussed over them from her chair. She was low on energy, it was obvious to see, so they resolved not to stay very long.

'Hey, Mama,' Elvis told her, and cradled her soft, tear-filled face in his hands. 'I told you everything would be all right.'

'I know,' she said. 'And it was, wasn't it? Everything was just fine.'

He was turning transparent before their eyes. He was see-through blue and silvery.

'Elvis … something's happening to you,' she said, huskily. 'It's like you're changing … into starlight …'

'I am, Mama,' he whispered. 'Didn't I always tell you I was going to be a star? It's what we're made from … in the end we all become stars …'

Mrs Presley smiled and nodded. And then she fell asleep and her visitors knew that she wouldn't wake up again.

The ghostly Elvis led them quietly, back through Graceland, back outside, to the TARDIS.

'Thank you, Doctor,' he said. 'I don't know why you let my mama and me keep those phones in the first place. And I know it was you, in a different form, somehow. I don't know how that works, but I know it was you. You tried to be kind, and then you had to put it all right. And I want to tell you – thank you. You've given me something I never would have had otherwise. I got to kiss her goodbye.'

The Doctor wrinkled her nose and gave a modest shrug. 'Hey, it was just me being my usual clumsy, interfering self.' She beamed at him. 'History hasn't quite gone back into its usual groove. There's still a couple of things awry. That business with Frank Sinatra isn't quite right in real-world terms, and your mum being at home when she died … well, that's a bit off-kilter, too. But I honestly think it's all better this way and not all that disastrous. I think we've actually managed to improve on history here today. And it's not every day you can say that!' Saying this, the Doctor stepped forward to hug the puzzled-looking Elvis …

And the old ghost faded away into nothingness.

The TARDIS team were standing alone on the grass outside Graceland and the moon was full in the Memphis skies.

'C'mon, Doc,' Graham told the unusually quiet Doctor. 'Maybe it's time we were on our way. Come on, guys.'

The Doctor took a deep breath. 'You're right. Let's go, fam.' And she grinned at the moon and the mansion with its soft golden lights, and the faint trace of stardust in the dark air.

Einstein and the Doctor

Jo Cotterill

The time rotor wheezed to a stop. 'Here we are!' announced the Doctor. 'Bern, Switzerland.' She peered at the display. 'Hmm. I was aiming for 1905 but I think we might be a bit earlier than that. The TARDIS sometimes has its own funny ideas.' She twisted a handle. 'Some odd readings here, wonder what's going on?'

'I can't believe we're going to meet Einstein,' Graham said, his eyes alight. 'What a legend.'

'Do we get to go to his wedding?' asked Yaz hopefully. 'After what you said at my nan's in 1947 ...'

'Certainly not,' the Doctor said firmly. 'I officiated at Albert's wedding. Well, another me. I can't bump into myself; it'd be embarrassing. I wouldn't know where to look.'

Ryan took the craziness in his stride as usual. 'Does Einstein have that mad hair, like on the posters?'

'Depends how much he's been drinking,' remarked the Doctor, tucking the sonic into her pocket. 'He's a right party animal, old Bertie.'

Yaz gave Ryan a gentle punch. 'Oi, it's not just his hair he's famous for; it's his brain.'

'Too right,' said the Doctor. 'Did you know he left his brain to science? When they cut it up, they discovered that his inferior parietal lobe was fifteen per cent wider than a normal person's.'

Graham stared at her. 'Inferior what?'

'They cut up his *brain*?' Ryan pulled a face. 'That's disgusting.'

'I think it's amazing,' Yaz countered. 'He was still contributing to science, even after death.'

They stepped out of the TARDIS into a park, the door clicking shut behind them.

'Brrr. Seems to be winter.' The Doctor gazed around. Straight, neat footpaths bordered grassy squares, but no feet crunched the stones. An ornate ironwork bandstand rose empty from the other side of the dark still duckpond. The trees, twisted and bare, traced black lines against the white sky. No birds perched in the branches. 'Not exactly lively, is it? Where is everyone?'

'There.' Ryan pointed. Coming in through the corner gate was a couple, their steps quick and hurried, their breath puffing into the air. The woman wore a headscarf tied tightly under her chin; her arms were crossed over her chest in the cold. The man at her side wore a hat pulled low over his forehead and carried what looked like a large bundle of blankets. They hurried onwards, gazes fixed firmly on the ground.

'What's he carrying?' Yaz took a step forward.

'Laundry?' suggested Graham.

'A child,' said the Doctor, her voice calm and quiet.

As the couple neared, the four travellers could see two legs dangling from the bundle, short socks and girls' shoes encasing the feet. No one said anything until the Doctor stepped forward to intercept. 'Good afternoon,' she said.

The couple started violently, the woman letting out a stifled shriek.

'I'm sorry, I didn't mean to startle you,' the Doctor went on. 'We've just arrived here. Seeing the sights of Bern, you know.'

'Friedrich, we mustn't stop,' the woman said, her voice high and tight. 'Johanna …'

The man shifted his arms, and the blanket slipped sideways, revealing a small golden head. The girl's eyes were closed, and there was a bluish pallor to her skin.

'Johanna? Is this your daughter?' asked the Doctor. She reached out a hand to brush the girl's hair out of her face, but Friedrich jerked back.

'Don't touch her!'

'What's wrong with her?' asked Yaz.

Friedrich glared at her. 'Same thing that's wrong with all the others. Marthe, come.' He and the woman turned to set off again.

'Where are you taking her?' the Doctor called after them.

'Where do you think?' Friedrich snapped back. 'To get help!' He jerked his head to where a tall gothic spire rose out of the trees.

'From the church?' asked Yaz. 'Why not the hospital?' But the couple ignored the question as they hurried out of the park, Johanna's head lolling lifelessly.

'All the others?' repeated Graham. 'What others?'

The Doctor raised her eyebrows. 'Looks like we'll be taking a little detour on our way to Mr Einstein.'

The four of them stood in the square in front of the cathedral and gazed up.

'Whoa,' said Ryan.

The sandstone edifice of Berner Münster towered over the city, its octagonal bell tower a full hundred metres high. The enormous central entrance arch was flanked by two smaller ones, pleasingly symmetrical, and the whole building was decorated with ornate swirls and crenellations. Inside the central arch, over a hundred tiny stone figures decorated with gilt were frozen in a scene from the Last Judgement.

'Only completed a decade ago,' said the Doctor. 'Bit fancy for me.'

'Hello!' called a uniformed man standing in the doorway of the cathedral. 'All are welcome; please come in.'

'Police,' the Doctor noted, strolling over. 'Why's there a police officer on the door of a holy place?'

The man looked surprised. 'To keep order. With so many people coming …' He spread his hands. 'There are ten of us here. Officers have been posted on all the churches in the city. Haven't you seen the papers?'

'We've just arrived,' said Yaz.

'Come in, come in!' the officer called to someone over Yaz's shoulder. A woman holding a baby was crossing the square. She looked up at the sound – and then her gaze jerked higher, and she stopped dead, staring, her mouth opening into a high, terrified scream.

'What's she seen?' The Doctor and her friends ran back out into the middle of the square and swung round, looking up.

'I don't see ...' Graham's words trailed away.

Silhouetted against the cold white sky, a huge creature now crouched on the cathedral roof. As they watched, one long brown leg covered in hairs extended itself, followed by another, and another, and the thick brown body rose slightly with the movement. Multiple black eyes shone above pointed mandibles, opening and closing convulsively.

'Not again!' said Ryan, swallowing.

'Where'd it come from?' Yaz glanced around nervously.

'Giant spider. Interesting.' The Doctor aimed the sonic at it and then pursed her lips at the readout. 'Ooh. *That's* interesting too.' She stepped forward and called up to the giant arachnid. 'Oi! You and me need to have a little talk.'

The eight eyes swivelled in her direction.

'I'm the Doctor. And you are?'

The enormous hairy body hesitated. And then with one swift movement, it gathered its legs and leaped, mandibles open and ready.

'Doctor!' yelled Yaz.

The spider fell towards the Doctor – and passed right through her. As it reached the ground, the supposedly solid body splashed silently into smoke, blew up into the air, and drifted away.

In a matter of seconds, the entire creature had disappeared.

The Doctor coughed and brushed an imaginary speck off her shoulder. Then she pocketed the sonic. 'Totally knew that would happen,' she said to herself. She grinned brightly at the woman on the other side of the square, still frozen in fear. 'Don't worry! Just a hallucination from all the stress you're under!' She turned to the others and used a pantomime whisper: 'D'you think she believed me?'

The woman crossed herself and hurried towards the cathedral, avoiding the Doctor and her companions.

'If we're doing giant spiders again, I'm going home,' said Ryan. 'Once was enough.'

'Wasn't a spider,' said the Doctor, shaking her head. 'Just looked like one. Actually, it was—'

A high terrified wail came from inside the cathedral, making everyone jump again.

'It's going to be one of *those* days, isn't it?' Graham said wearily.

The interior of the cathedral was just as impressive as its exterior. The crisscrossed stone ceiling looked down on a long nave ending in the choir and six stunning stained-glass windows. Stone pillars divided the nave from two side aisles, which opened on to several chapels. The cavernous space was filled with soft noises from the hundreds of people who had sought sanctuary here.

'Oh …' Yaz said quietly.

It was hard to register the sheer scale of the view. The pews and chairs were filled, and the mass of humanity spilled out into the aisles, the chapels, the choir. Everywhere Yaz looked, she could see people huddled together, weeping, praying, rocking. And held by the adults, smaller bodies, with closed eyes and pale lips. Lolling heads and limp limbs.

'The children,' breathed the Doctor beside her. 'Look at the children.'

'Dear God.' Graham's voice was barely a whisper.

Their faces all had the bluish pallor of Johanna, the girl they had seen in the park. Their chests moved slightly on each inhalation, but there was no other sign of life.

'Why aren't they in the hospital?' Ryan said, his voice harsh in the subdued atmosphere.

'Because the doctors have failed us,' came a bitter reply.

'Friedrich,' said Yaz, recognising the man from the park. He and his wife Marthe were sitting against a wall, Johanna lain across their laps.

'What do you mean, the doctors have failed you?' The Doctor crouched down beside them.

'When it started, it was just a few children falling ill,' Friedrich said. 'Then it spread and spread. Now every street has a sick child – everyone is terrified. The doctors say they can't find anything wrong! They are worse than useless. I wouldn't let a single doctor near my child.'

The Doctor glanced at her friends. 'Maybe they don't know what they're looking for.'

Marthe's eyes narrowed. 'Who are you?' she asked suspiciously. 'You're not from Bern.'

'No,' said the Doctor. 'We only arrived today. Thought we'd drop in on an old friend. That's Graham, Ryan, and Yaz. And I'm the – er.' She stopped. 'I'm Rose.'

'Well, you picked the wrong day to come to Bern, Rose,' Friedrich told her.

Johanna whimpered slightly, her eyes flickering under their lids. Marthe clutched her hand. 'I wish we knew how to help her.'

'It doesn't affect adults?' asked Ryan.

Friedrich shook his head. 'Only the little ones. The innocents.' His gaze travelled over to the grand altar at the other end of the nave.

'Of course,' said the Doctor, understanding. 'When science fails …'

'Only God can help us,' Friedrich said.

The Doctor patted Johanna's head then got to her feet, hands in her pockets. The others followed her into the shadows.

'This is heartbreaking,' Graham said quietly.

Ryan nodded. 'D'you think it's got anything to do with the giant spider?'

'Told you, it wasn't a giant spider,' the Doctor said. 'It was made of energy, not mass. That's why it vanished when it hit the floor. It wasn't actually solid.'

'*Ghost* spiders?' Yaz shuddered. 'Makes it *so* much better.'

'Will there be more?' asked Graham.

'I've no idea,' said the Doctor. 'But we can't find out from in here. We need to scope out the area, take some readings. Doctor stuff.'

'Thought your name was Rose,' Graham said with a small smile.

'Couldn't call myself "Doctor", could I? Not after what Friedrich just said. Rose was the first name that popped into my head.' The Doctor cleared her throat. 'Graham and Ryan, I need you to stay here and keep an eye on things. Do what you can to help.'

Ryan nodded. 'Right.'

'Yaz and I will see what we can find out in the city,' the Doctor went on. 'The TARDIS picked up some unusual energy readings, and that ghost spider was a match.'

'Fine time to meet up with your pal Bertie,' said Graham.

'Isn't it, though!' The Doctor grinned. 'Something science can't explain? This is right up Albert's street! Literally, in this case. He lives just round the corner.'

The late afternoon light was weakening as Yaz followed the Doctor down the near-empty Münstergasse. 'Keep your eyes and ears open,' the Doctor instructed. She held out the sonic and swept her arm in a wide circle. 'There's a lot of low-level energy noise here; I can't work out where it's coming from. It keeps changing, too. Look everywhere, Yaz – up, down, sideways.'

Yaz felt her senses heightening. Danger could come from any angle; her police training had taught her that, and life with the Doctor had proved it a hundred times over. Her adrenalin spiked as they passed the University Library and a door slammed open. Several men spilled out onto the street, laughing.

'A giant spider, I'm telling you,' one of them was saying. 'Crawling up the street. Must have been twenty feet tall.'

'How much beer have you had, Heinz?' Another man punched him playfully on the shoulder.

'Georg saw it too,' insisted Heinz. 'Tell them, Georg.'

Georg, blond and bespectacled, looked uncomfortable. 'I don't know *what* I saw. But there must be a scientific explanation.'

'Excuse me.' The Doctor didn't stand on ceremony. 'A giant spider, you say?'

Heinz stared at her. 'Yes. About half an hour ago. It came up the street here, and then it vanished.'

The others roared with laughter.

'What happened when it vanished?' asked the Doctor.

Heinz shrugged. 'Don't know. It turned into a kind of smoke. Then it just blew away.'

'Exactly what happened to us!' the Doctor exclaimed to Yaz. 'The same thing in two different places, and at around the same time it sounds like. Curiouser and curiouser, as I once said to my old pal Charlie Dodgson. Which way did the smoke go, Heinz?'

Heinz pointed and, with a hurried thanks, the Doctor and Yaz set off again.

'Even energy has to go somewhere,' the Doctor said to Yaz. 'If we can find the source …'

They reached the end of the street, the Doctor scanning as they went, and turned into Kramgasse, stepping over the tram lines that ran down the centre. Solid stone walls rose up impressively either side of the road. On the ground floor were arcades fronting shop windows. Above were the tall rectangular windows of apartments, rising to three storeys. This was clearly a busy shopping and trading area on a normal day, but today only a handful of people were around, talking soberly in small groups, or glancing fearfully from side to side as they went. There were no children in sight. One woman was being comforted by a friend, her tear-streaked face telling its own story.

'Things are really bad,' Yaz said.

The Doctor nodded grimly. 'It'll be good to get Albert's take on this. He always sees things differently. Nearly there now – number 49.'

Yaz followed the Doctor under an arch and up a very narrow spiral staircase to the second floor. Here there was a simple door with a knocker and the handwritten label 'Einstein' at head height.

The Doctor reached for the knocker and then paused. Voices could be heard from inside – loud, angry voices.

'It was just a spider!' a woman was shouting. 'You're being ridiculous!'

'It was deadly!' a man cried back. 'I've read about them. They can kill within seconds!'

'It's a *house* spider, Albert, we get them all the time. I am *not* contacting the police to tell them you've imagined up a poisonous spider.'

'Show them the body!' Albert screamed. 'Then they'll see!'

The Doctor and Yaz glanced at each other with raised eyebrows. 'A spider?' murmured the Doctor. Then she knocked loudly.

The voices inside stopped abruptly. Footsteps came, and the door opened into a small hallway. A woman stood there, flustered and self-conscious. She had a soft round face and dark hair swept back from her forehead into a loose bun. 'Yes?'

'Mileva, good to see you again!' The Doctor stepped forward to embrace her.

The woman jerked back. 'Who are you?'

The Doctor laughed apologetically. 'Of course, you haven't met this face before. Sorry. I was at your wedding.'

'What?' Mileva glanced uneasily down the hallway. 'I'm not married. Yet.'

'You're not? Ah!' The Doctor turned to Yaz. 'This is just *before* the wedding I told you about. We're cutting it a bit fine, I must say.' She beamed at Mileva. 'We're, uh, friends – well, at this point, colleagues – of your fiancé. I'm the Doctor and this is Yaz.'

'This is not a good time.'

'No, but it's the right time.' The Doctor smiled hopefully. 'Whatever's going on, I'm pretty sure we can help.'

Mileva gave an exasperated shrug. 'You'd better come in. I would say excuse the mess, but it's always like this.'

Indeed, the small sitting room they were ushered into was covered in piles of paper with handwritten notes, textbooks, bits of scientific apparatus, and pots of ink.

Twitching in a corner, looking at the same time aggressive and terrified, was a short man with slicked-back hair. His moustache looked somewhat hopeful rather than impressive.

Yaz's jaw dropped. 'Is that him? He doesn't look anything like his picture!'

'Who are you? What's going on?' The man had a round face like the woman, though his eyes were fiercer. 'Are you from the police? I need to report a dangerous animal.'

'The Doctor and Yaz,' said Mileva patiently. 'They are colleagues of yours, from England, I think?'

'Near enough,' said the Doctor.

Albert's eyes narrowed. 'I don't recognise them.'

'Are you working on one of your Theories?' Yaz reached out to a pile of papers.

'Don't touch that!' Albert snapped out. 'I *was* working, until I was attacked by a deadly arachnid.'

'What happened to it?' asked the Doctor.

'I can show you!' Albert said triumphantly. 'It happened not half an hour ago. I kept its body – look!' He held out a glass jar, lid tightly closed. Inside was the curled over body of a large but common house spider. 'I killed it!' Albert announced. 'You can see the venom dripping from its fangs, ready to inject into me!'

The Doctor and Yaz peered at the body. There were no fangs, no venom. The Doctor flicked a glance at Yaz. 'Gosh,' she said. 'You had a lucky escape there, Mr Einstein. Looks like an *Arachne fatalis mendax* to me. We'll take this back to the lab and run some tests on it.' She pocketed the jar.

Albert seemed to relax. 'Good, good,' he said, nodding. 'Excellent. Need to find out if there are any more of these around. There could be an infestation. And that reminds me.' He stiffened as he looked back to Mileva. 'I heard a rat.'

'We've been over this, sweetheart,' Mileva said gently.

'I did!' Albert ran his hand through his hair so that it stuck up in tufts. A feverish light appeared in his eyes. 'I heard it in the walls.' As Mileva reached out to pat Albert on the arm, he recoiled. 'Your wrist! What is that on your skin?'

Puzzled, Mileva held up her hand. 'Nothing. A small burn from the iron yesterday.'

'Blisters,' Albert insisted. 'Red, weeping – you should see a doctor. You!' He swung round to his visitors. 'One of you is a doctor! Look at her – can't you see the disease eating through the skin?'

Mileva's lip trembled. 'Albert – darling …'

'Why don't you come into the kitchen and show me?' suggested the Doctor. 'Then I can clean it if I need to.'

Albert nodded. 'Yes. It looks contagious.'

The Doctor ushered Mileva out of the room and Yaz followed. Tears were flowing down Mileva's face. In the tiny kitchen, she held up her wrist. 'See, just a small red mark! He is imagining it all!'

The Doctor nodded. 'Something's badly wrong with him.' She pulled the jar out of her pocket. 'Bit of a coincidence that Albert was hallucinating about a deadly spider around the time we saw one outside the cathedral.'

A door slammed. Mileva whipped round. 'Albert!' They heard footsteps going down the stairs outside.

'Best to let him go for now,' said the Doctor. 'I could do with taking some readings.' She went back through to the sitting room and started scanning with the sonic. 'Hmm. Hardly anything here now …'

Yaz helped a sobbing Mileva to a chair. 'We've come through so much already,' said Mileva, a handkerchief clutched to her face. 'How can we marry if he's not in his right mind? He'll have to go home. His mother at least will be pleased,' she added bitterly.

'His mother?' Yaz moved some books off a nearby chair and sat down next to her.

Mileva sniffed. 'She's always hated me. She wants Albert to marry a nice German girl, and I'm Serbian. But love is what it is, no? You cannot choose where your heart finds its home. And I have loved him since we met. Since we took the same Physics class at the Polytechnic.' She looked up at a photograph on the wall that showed the two of them together. 'Six years ago. Six long years, and so often apart. When we were together, we were like molecules bonding. When apart, we shared our minds in letters. We even had pet names for each other.' She looked down at her hands. 'He is my soulmate.'

'I'm sure he'll come round,' Yaz said softly. 'And I *know* you'll be married. Right, Doctor?'

But the Doctor was pulling a face. 'Only if things work out as they should here,' she said. 'The future could change. It's all relative, space and time.' She looked sharply at Mileva. 'Forget you heard that.'

But Mileva was distracted by a sound from outside. 'What's that?' She went to the window and pulled it open. The three of them leaned out over the ledge to look down into the street, where a dark cloud was growing. A skittering sound could be heard.

The Doctor pulled out the sonic which buzzed. 'It's the same energy that made the spider! Only, it's much stronger ...'

'It's not a spider this time,' said Yaz.

Mileva shuddered. 'That sound ...'

The skittering was getting louder. There was a metallic tang to the sound that set their teeth on edge. A handful of people were hurrying away from it, glancing nervously behind.

The black cloud rippled and shivered and solidified…

'Rats,' breathed Mileva, her hands clutching convulsively at the ledge. 'A river of rats.'

Now they could see she was right, as the torrent poured up the street towards them. Thousands of small dark bodies, with teeth chittering and sharp claws scratching stone. One man stood still in the middle of the street, a loaf of bread in his arms, his gaze fixed in horror at the oncoming sight.

'Sir!' the Doctor yelled down. 'Run!'

'Is he in danger?' Yaz asked. 'The spider didn't hurt you.'

'The readings on this are much higher! Please, sir – RUN!'

The man turned to look up at them but he was already out of time. The river simply swallowed him up with a horrible, moist chewing and tearing.

'Oh, God!' Up on the second floor, Mileva covered her mouth, her eyes wide and horrified. Yaz turned away, sickened. The Doctor gripped the ledge, white-knuckled, her mouth a tight line, until it was all over – until the rats had passed down the street, leaving only a grisly twisted skeleton behind them. 'I'm so sorry,' she breathed.

Then a plume of black smoke rose up from somewhere in the next street. The Doctor snapped into action. 'Come on! We've got to follow it! Get downstairs as quick as you can!'

Never had a cathedral been home to such great fear and so many pleading prayers. Everywhere Graham looked, adults clutched and rocked their silent children, faces raised to heaven, lips whispering endless Our Fathers. Candles flickered in every holder, casting shadows over already drawn faces, making them skull-like in the dimness. At the altar, the bishop was holding a service. Murmured prayers flitted across the stone-ribbed ceiling like sparrows. Further away from the Choir, it was harder to hear the service, not only because of the distance but because of other conversations, whispered and agitated, occasionally rising into a confrontation. 'Why aren't you *doing* anything?' one man was repeating at a police officer stationed by a side chapel. 'This is a national emergency, and you're just standing there!'

'I'm sorry, sir,' the officer responded. 'We're just here to keep the peace.'

'To watch our children die, more like,' said the man furiously. Hands grabbed him and urged him away. Graham and Ryan breathed a sigh of relief as he capitulated. The officer looked down at the floor.

'All these people ...' Graham said quietly, 'and no one to help them.'

'The Doctor will,' said Ryan.

'Yeah, but she's not here, is she?' Graham looked around. 'I feel so useless.'

A sudden flurry of activity by the main entrance distracted them. Six people were stumbling in, three children carried between them. The adults were all white-faced, their words clattering out of them: 'Rats! Rats everywhere! Thousands of them!'

Graham and Ryan made their way over. 'What did you say?' asked Ryan. 'Rats?'

A woman tugged on his jacket. 'They chased us down the street!' she said, her breath stinging his face. 'My sister Aiga … she fell … and they … they *ate* her.' She stopped, appalled at her own words. 'They ate her,' she repeated, bewildered – and then burst into tears.

Ryan patted her awkwardly as Graham peered out into the empty square. 'Where did you see these rats?'

'They've gone now,' one of the men said. In his arms he held a boy of about two, eyes closed, skin blue around the lips. 'They were nearly on us, and then they just … I don't know. Vanished. One minute they were there, the next they were gone.'

'Like the spider,' Graham said to Ryan.

He nodded. 'Only the rats killed someone.' He and Graham helped the new arrivals find somewhere to settle on the end of a pew and then withdrew to a side aisle. 'I need to do something; I'm going mad here. The Doctor told us to help.'

'Help how, though?' wondered Graham, pulling up the zip of his jacket. 'It's getting colder. These people could use some warming up. Blankets or something.'

'Curtains – or them frocks the priests wear?' said Ryan.

'Good thinking. Maybe the bishop has a stash of biscuits somewhere. And there must be a water tap, we can make some drinks. Every little helps, right? Grab a candle. Let's get to work.'

The Doctor raced down the street, sonic held out like a divining rod. Mileva and Yaz followed along behind, turning right then left, left again, then …

'Oh blast!' The Doctor swung the sonic in a wide arc, trying to get a fix. 'The signal's disappeared! Too weak! Or too fast for us. One or the other. Maybe I can change the settings, try to expand the range.' She bopped the sonic several times, which made a protesting noise.

'What's that?' asked Yaz suddenly.

'What's what?' asked Mileva.

Yaz was staring at the wall of a nearby shop. Smooth grey stone – she ran her hand over it. 'I saw something here, just for a sec, and then it … oh!' She pulled back her hand in shock. 'There's something there. Invisible.'

'Invisible?' said the Doctor, immediately intrigued. She ran her hand over the surface. 'You're absolutely right, Yaz. There's something here, stuck to the wall. Something … squidgy.'

'I'm sure I saw it,' said Yaz. 'Just for a second, when you were waving the sonic around.'

The Doctor directed the sonic at the wall. Clinging to the smooth stone was something small and star-shaped that pulsed and quivered with energy.

'What in heaven's name is that?' asked Mileva. Her hand reached for the cross she wore around her neck.

'I don't know,' said the Doctor, 'but it's beautiful. Look at the way the light ripples across its skin.'

'It's like a sort of starfish,' said Yaz, gazing at it. 'How come we can see it now?'

The Doctor checked the settings on the sonic. 'Ultraviolet. I must have switched it on by accident.' She swung the beam away from the small creature, and it vanished. She swung it back, and the illuminated star reappeared. 'It's only visible in ultraviolet light.'

Mileva stared at the sonic. 'You can create ultraviolet light without a vapour lamp? What is that device?'

'Oh, standard issue back at my lab,' said the Doctor carelessly. She peered more closely at the creature. 'What are you then, my squishy?' She prodded it gently. 'So light and soft, you can hardly feel it.'

'Look!' Mileva pointed as another starfish came floating gently through the air as though caught in a current, bumping into the stone, spiralling slowly to rest next to the first.

'They can fly!' Yaz was amazed. 'How many are there?

'There could be thousands,' mused Mileva. 'How would we know if we cannot see them? Perhaps they belong to an entire invisible realm, evolving alongside our own over millions of years.'

'Or on another world. Look out!' The Doctor took a step backwards as two more starfish came drifting through the air to settle beside the others. 'I wonder what's attracting them?'

'And why use a colour beyond the visible spectrum?' added Mileva. 'Perhaps it is a kind of camouflage? To avoid predators? Or because they *are* predators?'

The starfish pulsed in time with her words. Another one drifted down to join the little cluster.

'They glow more when we talk,' said the Doctor, fascinated. 'Do they feed on words?'

'Or thoughts,' suggested Yaz.

The Doctor let out a yelp that startled the others. 'Yaz! You're brilliant! Thoughts! Imaginative energy!' She turned to Mileva. 'Go on, have some more ideas. That beautiful mind of yours, working out what they could be.'

Mileva looked puzzled. 'I was merely speculating … we still know so little about the spectrum of light. For example, there are creatures under the sea that create their own light by phosphorescence. Phosphorescent materials absorb light and then emit it very slowly. It's how radioactivity was discovered. I read all the papers on it.' She became enthused. 'It makes me wonder if we could find a way to transmit light waves through various solid objects, through changing the wave forms or …'

'Look,' whispered the Doctor. More and more starfish were floating towards them, so close they were bumping into each other on their way. 'That's it!' She turned to Mileva. 'You're using your imagination. Every time you have an idea, more of them come. *That's* what's happening!'

'Sounds like a children's story.' Yaz shook her head, wondering. 'Magic starfish drawn to ideas?'

'Children!' exclaimed the Doctor, slapping her own forehead. 'Yaz, you're full of brilliant ideas today!'

'I am?' Yaz rubbed her eyes. 'Not sure how. I'm knackered.'

Mileva leaned against the wall, pressing her fingers to her temples. 'I too. So tired, and my head aches.' She slid down the wall to sit on the cold cobblestones. Yaz joined her. The Doctor crouched down, concerned. 'You feel tired?'

'Like lead,' murmured Yaz.

'Can't … think any more …' said Mileva, her eyes closing.

'This explains EVERYTHING!' the Doctor cried, jolting the other two awake again. 'Well, not *everything*

everything, but some of it. The starfish, and the children, and the energy readings …' She switched settings on the sonic and pointed it at Mileva and Yaz. 'Yes, the same thing! The energy is coming from *humans* – your imaginations! It's being sucked out of you, by these tiny critters!' She beamed.

'That … doesn't make me feel better,' Yaz said, squeezing her eyes shut.

'The starfish feed on imaginative energy,' the Doctor went on. 'And who has the most fertile imagination on the planet? Children. A new idea every ten seconds! Constantly questioning and wondering – a proper feast for a hungry magic starfish. No wonder the poor kids are all collapsing. Young minds can't cope with so much energy being siphoned off.' She frowned at the wall of glowing creatures. 'We can't have this, you know. You can't just come in here and suck stuff out of people; it's illegal. Those children are going to die if you don't leave them alone.'

'So tired …' murmured Mileva.

'Mileva?' A voice made them all look up. Albert stood in the street, hair no longer carefully combed back, jacket collar ripped, arms hanging loosely at his sides. 'My darling, is that you?'

'Albert!' With a sob, Mileva heaved herself to her feet and lurched into his arms. 'I was so worried about you! What happened?'

Albert held her for a moment and then put her gently away from him. 'I found the rat,' he said, his eyes taking on the feverish gleam they had seen before. 'I found all the rats, Mileva! I told you I could hear them.'

'Look at his hands,' the Doctor said quietly to Yaz. 'They're trembling.'

'They're not normal rats, Mileva,' Albert went on. 'They're twice the size. I think something has happened to them. They've evolved into killers. We have to tell people! We have to have the streets cleansed!'

Mileva sagged. 'Albert, no, not again ...'

The Doctor pointed the sonic at Einstein. 'The readouts are off the scale!' she said to Yaz. 'The energy is just *pouring* out of him.' She shone the ultraviolet beam on the wall. They both gasped. The wall was now completely covered with starfish, and they were pulsing brighter and faster than ever before.

'It's like he's charging them up,' said Yaz, astonished. 'Like he's some kind of human battery.'

'That oversized parietal lobe of his! They're getting the best feast of their lives,' the Doctor agreed. 'Trouble is—'

'You don't believe me!' Albert said to Mileva. He took a step backwards. 'You think I'm going mad, don't you? I can see it in your eyes!'

'I don't know what to think!' Mileva wailed. 'All I know is, you're not yourself.'

'I'm not myself?' Albert repeated. His eyebrows lowered and he stepped forward again. 'What if *you're* not yourself? What if you're not who I thought you were, Mileva? Are you the sweet Dollie I used to write to, or are you someone else?'

'Stop it, Albert, you're frightening me!'

The light emanating from the starfish began to darken into an intense fiery glow.

'You never wanted to marry me,' Albert said, his voice dropping to a menacing growl. 'You just wanted to steal the ideas out of my head to further your own work.'

Mileva gasped. 'How can you say that? You know I love you more than my own life!'

The skies were already gloomy with twilight; now an extra darkness settled around them; a whirling blackness. The Doctor looked up, alarmed. 'Albert, stop it.'

'What's happening?' asked Yaz.

'The starfish don't seem to make Albert tired,' the Doctor told her. 'If anything, he's creating even *more* energy – but it's damaging him. Like, I don't know, an allergic reaction. It's changing his personality – and all this extra energy is too much for the starfish to absorb, so it's taking a darker path …'

Behind Einstein the black cloud began to take shape: a tall, monstrous figure with a voluminous skirt, dark hair and a round face …

'It's Mileva,' gulped Yaz.

Mileva screamed in horror. 'Albert, no!'

'Albert, you have to stop!' called the Doctor. 'Can't you see what your fears are creating?'

Einstein turned around and quailed at the giant figure glaring down at him. 'It's not my fault! She's in on it! Her, and my mother, and my colleagues at work! They're all trying to destroy me!' More giant figures started to form in the smoke, open angry mouths and reaching arms. A chimney pot was swiped from a nearby roof and smashed into the street, sending shards flying. The figures started to move closer, huge smoky shoes cracking the stones beneath their feet.

'Doctor . . .' said Yaz nervously.

'Yes,' said the Doctor. 'That's quite enough.' She twisted the sonic again and pointed it directly at Einstein's head. 'Sorry.' She pressed the button. Albert's eyes rolled back in his head and he fainted clean away, folding onto the cobblestones like a marionette with its strings cut. Instantly, the looming figures collapsed too, the dark smoke puddling on the ground and flowing back into Albert like black mercury.

'Bertie equals monsters squared,' the Doctor murmured.

Mileva was kneeling next to her fiancé, cradling his head and stroking his hair. 'My darling, what has happened to you? How can I save you?'

The Doctor gazed at her for a moment. 'You're an incredible woman, Mileva. How much are you willing to risk to help save him?'

Mileva looked up at her, eyes blazing. 'Everything.'

The Doctor nodded. 'Then, in the few minutes we have before he wakes up, we need to talk. Yaz, come and plonk yourself down. It's Plan Time.'

There was a surprising amount of cloth in the cathedral once they started to collect it. Surplices, cassocks, chasubles, veils, curtains, mufflers for the bell clappers . . .

Once the police understood what Graham and Ryan were suggesting, they took charge of the situation, marshalling volunteers into a chain, passing out extra materials and carrying out their own searches for more food. More and more candles were lit, providing small globes of light around the cavernous hall. Outside, a slice of moon was rising in the clear sky, casting a pale gleam through the tall windows in the choir vault at the east end.

Ryan cursed as he fell down the last few steps of the bell tower, dropping his bundle and spilling hot candle wax onto his hands. 'I hate stairs.'

'Look what I found!' Graham brandished a wooden box triumphantly. 'Marzipan!' He passed it to a man at the end of a pew, who took it gratefully.

'I have not eaten since yesterday,' he said. 'Thank you.' He took one sweet out of the box and gave it to his wife. Then he took one for himself and passed the box along to the next family.

'That'll only be enough for a few people,' Ryan said.

'But those few people will feel better for it,' Graham pointed out. 'Besides, haven't you heard the story about the loaves and the fishes?'

'We ain't got any of those,' Ryan said.

'No …' Graham watched the box as it was passed along from person to person, each taking only one sweet, 'but you watch …'

People started to open their bags, to pull out wafers, dried meat, bread rolls. The marzipan was soon gone, but the box kept going. Nearly everyone who took something out of it put something back in. Soon the box was fuller than it had been to start with.

'People take,' Graham said quietly, 'but they give back more. That's what the loaves and fishes were all about.'

'Graham?' Marthe had made her way over to them. Her face was strained. 'Johanna … she's getting worse.

We've been giving her sips of water, but now … Will you come?'

They followed her back to Friedrich, who still held the unconscious child across his knees. He looked up at them, fear in his eyes. 'She sounds like she can't catch her breath. Listen.'

Graham bent over, and could hear the breath stuttering in Johanna's throat. Her eyes no longer flickered under their lids, and when he felt for her pulse, it was weak and trembling.

'Is she … dying?' asked Marthe, her own voice catching on the last word.

Graham said helplessly, 'I don't know.' He placed his hand over the other man's. 'Don't give up hope. Our friends out there are trying to help, I promise.'

'*You* are helping,' said Marthe quietly. She took Graham's other hand. 'If you say there is still hope, then that gives us strength. We will try to believe.'

'So let me get this straight,' Yaz said, rubbing her head. 'You're going to try to lure all the starfish into one place, and trap them?'

'In a nutshell.' The Doctor nodded. 'Well, not *literally* a nutshell, that'd be far too small.'

'How do you plan to lure them?' Mileva asked, puzzled.

'Bait.' The Doctor looked at Einstein.

Yaz's jaw dropped. 'You're joking. You know what happens when he gets near those creatures!'

The Doctor nodded. 'Trouble is, they're drawn to him, aren't they? Way more than to any of the rest of us. His brain's unique, processing sensory information faster than anyone else's.'

Yaz raised an eyebrow. 'Faster than yours?'

'The starfish have developed a taste for *human* thought,' said the Doctor. 'Anyway we can't risk leaving him somewhere else. We need to make sure we get every last one of these brain-suckers, so we can take them somewhere safe.'

'Where would be safe?' asked Yaz.

'I'll find somewhere,' said the Doctor. 'It's a big universe.'

'No,' said Mileva. She was shaking her head mutinously. 'I can't allow you to use him like that. It could make his mind collapse completely.' She clutched the unconscious Albert to her breast. 'What would I do without him?'

The Doctor looked at her kindly. 'You said you'd be willing to risk everything.'

'Not him! *I* can bring the starfish – use me!' Mileva insisted. 'My brain is as good as his, sometimes better. We have worked together for years. Many of his research papers he worked on with me.'

'He did?' Yaz stared. 'Then why isn't your name on them?'

'Because I am a woman,' said Mileva, as though it were obvious. 'You think they would allow a *female* mathematician to publish a scientific theory? You are living in a different world.'

'You don't know how true that is,' said Yaz.

'I can't use you,' the Doctor explained. 'Look how drained you were after only a few minutes. You'd lose consciousness. Albert is the only one who can produce the amount of energy we need.'

Albert began to stir.

'He's waking up,' said the Doctor. 'We haven't got much time. Mileva, you said you knew of somewhere we could go? We need somewhere spacious. Indoor, preferably, with windows. Big empty room.'

'The Rathaus,' said Mileva. 'It's not far from our apartment.'

'Town hall!' exclaimed the Doctor. 'Perfect! You get Albert there, Mileva and wait for us outside. Yaz and I will pick up some bits and pieces from the flat and join you as soon as we can. By the way, have you got a gramophone with one of those big trumpet thingies on top?'

'Yes, why?'

'I'll need it for the amplifier.'

Albert's eyes opened. 'Where am I?'

'You're with me, darling,' Mileva assured him. 'I'll look after you. Can you stand?' She helped him to his feet, and they staggered away.

'Doctor,' said Yaz in a low voice, 'if Albert is awake and we bring all those starfish in – thousands of them – then …'

The Doctor nodded. 'Yep. The ghosts will come too. Lots and lots of them. They'll flood the city. People will be in danger. That's why we have to work *really* fast, Yaz. Else there might not be a city to save.'

Yaz was thankful that the race to the Einsteins' apartment was without incident. The Doctor was like a whirlwind, picking up all sorts of bits and pieces from the various rooms and thrusting them into Yaz's arms. 'Copper wire, pliers, ooh, hammer and nails, you never know, hold that, Yaz – kitchen, kitchen … forks! Yes – and a big metal saucepan. Does this fit on your head, Yaz? No, not quite. Never mind, found a bigger one, hold this – oh, you can't – well, put some of the other things inside it …'

Yaz followed, trying not to drop anything. The Doctor wrenched the horn from the top of the gramophone with a grimace. 'Got everything?'

'Er …'

'Good! Let's go.'

They dashed back down the stairs, narrowly missing an elderly woman coming out of the flat below. 'Hey, watch out!'

'Sorry!' the Doctor said breathlessly. 'Got to save Einstein!'

'Tell him he's behind on his rent!' the woman shouted back.

They ran down the street, taking a left at the end. 'I remember the Rathaus,' the Doctor puffed. 'Smart building, got a double staircase outside, like a big triangle. You can run up one side and down the other, brilliant!'

Yaz glanced behind and gulped. 'Doctor, what's that?'

The moon overhead was casting shadows into the street. Some of the shadows seemed to be growing …

'Better speed up,' said the Doctor.

They found Mileva helping Albert up one of the stone staircases of the imposing Rathaus. 'Come on,' she was saying. 'It's only a little graze. You'll be fine.'

'What happened?' Yaz stopped as the Doctor ran ahead to open the enormous wooden doors with the sonic.

Albert turned burning eyes on Yaz. 'I fell,' he said, his voice taking on an added timbre of fear. 'Look.' He held out his arm, sleeve rolled back. From elbow to wrist there was a superficial graze.

'He tripped and scraped it on a wall,' Mileva explained.

'Looks sore,' said Yaz sympathetically.

'It is deep,' said Albert. 'Deeper than it looks. You can see the blood springing to the surface, there!'

Alarmed, Yaz looked at Mileva, who nodded. Again, Albert was seeing things that weren't there. 'Blood,' murmured Yaz, glancing at the street, where the shadows were stretching across the cobbles. Perhaps they weren't shadows after all ...

'Get inside, quick,' Yaz said, her arms aching from the weight of all the items she was carrying. The three of them made their way through the arched doorway into a gloomy hall and from there into a large vaulted room.

The Doctor, standing in the middle of the room, gave a sharp nod. 'Right, no time to lose. Yaz, bring all that stuff over here. Mileva, find a chair and put it in the middle of the room. Albert, sit on it and don't move.'

'The blood,' Albert muttered, examining his arm obsessively.

'Yaz, jam these forks into the gaps between the floorboards just here, with the prongs sticking up.' The Doctor pulled out the sonic and started untangling the copper wire.

Yaz knew by now not to ask questions when the Doctor was firing on all cylinders.

'Now open that big window as far as it'll go. And find me a big box.' Sparks flew from the sonic as the Doctor pointed it at the saucepan.

Mileva had dragged two chairs into the middle of the room, and was sitting firmly next to Albert, her hand possessively on his knee while he peered nervously at the graze on his arm. 'It's getting worse,' he said, his voice trembling. 'See the beads of blood forming? And this drip, down to my hand now?'

'My darling,' Mileva said. 'There are no beads, there is no drip. Look at me.' But Albert didn't hear her.

The Doctor had a look at her own handiwork. 'It's not perfect, but it'll do.' The large saucepan now had several copper wires fused to the outside, long coils of them trailing down to the floor. Positioned by the window was the horn from the gramophone. 'Here's a lovely hat for you, Albert.' She fitted the saucepan onto his head.

He reached up for it. 'What is this?'

'It's – an advanced machine for healing,' the Doctor improvised. 'It'll slow down that bleeding you're worried about.'

'Oh.' Albert subsided.

Yaz staggered back into the room, carrying a large empty tea chest. 'Is this big enough? Found it downstairs.'

'It'll have to do.' The Doctor examined it. 'Let's hope the starfish don't mind a game of Sardines. Now, all we have to do is wind these wires around the forks, and attach the ends to the trumpet thing.'

'We're amplifying Albert's brainwaves?' asked Yaz, winding wire around a fork.

'S'right. Need to make sure we can broadcast him right across the city. And the forks are to secure the wires so any pesky apparitions don't pull 'em out straight away.' She changed the settings on the sonic and plugged it into her handmade machine, so that the ultraviolet beam shone on the open window. 'Look at this!' The window frame was already covered in starfish, and more and more were floating in. 'Grab as many as you can and put them into the box. Mileva, you too. The aim of the game is to be the one who collects the most starfish and jams them into the box.'

'And to be alive at the end of it,' Yaz muttered.

The bishop had finished his service and begun another. More and more parents were glancing anxiously at their children, as the quiet regular breathing turned to tiny gasps. Instinctively, they moved forward, nearer the altar, craning to hear words of hope and comfort, even as many of them were losing hope themselves. Friedrich and Marthe were bent over Johanna, whispering prayer after prayer, telling her how much she was wanted and loved.

Graham was whispering his own prayer: 'Doctor, I wish you could hear me... we haven't got much time...'

Then there was a cry from the far end of the cathedral, and several hands pointed up at the giant windows. Something was seeping up the outside of the stained glass. Something thick and dark; something that moved like liquid but in the wrong direction.

Heads turned and prayers hushed. No one moved. Fear swept through the congregation as the moonlight dimmed.

'As if these people haven't been through enough,' Graham said, agonised.

'We should go and find the Doctor,' Ryan said.

A great heavy crashing sound echoed around the cathedral as the police closed the giant wooden doors, barring them firmly.

'Too late,' said Graham.

The starfish were pouring in at the window, and Albert was starting to shake in his chair. 'Look!' he gasped, holding out his arms. 'They're turning black! The blood is rotting in my veins!' He leaped up, the saucepan falling from his head, his hair springing into the characteristic Einstein look.

Mileva rushed back to him. 'Albert!'

'Stay calm,' ordered the Doctor.

Yaz, at the window, wrinkled her nose. 'What's that smell?' Seeping up the outside of the walls was the same black shadow that had followed them down the street. Only now it was easier to see. 'Blood! Doctor, the street outside is covered in blood! And it's coming up the walls!'

'Albert, please put this back on,' urged Mileva, holding out the saucepan, but he recoiled.

'Get away from me! You're behind all this, I know! You poisoned me! You set the spider on me!'

'Alllberrrtt!' A grinding, resonant voice came from the recesses of the hall, and the giant Mileva glided forward, arms reaching out as they had in the street earlier. 'Alllberrtt, come to meee!'

'Get away!' screamed Albert. 'Don't touch me!'

Another figure appeared from behind Mileva. 'Alllberrtt …'

'It looks like Michele Besso,' Mileva said, frightened. 'He's Albert's best friend.'

Albert backed away, holding out his hands as protection.

'Einstein thinks everyone's against him.' The Doctor grabbed the sonic and aimed it at the apparitions but nothing happened. 'I can't stop them – any of them!'

'What have you done to my son, Serbian witch?' hissed a new voice from the shadows.

'That sounds like Pauline.' Mileva turned ghostly pale. 'Albert's mother.'

All sound had ceased in the cathedral. Everyone who was still conscious was looking at the windows which lined three sides of the building. Outside was dark, but it was still possible to discern the unknown liquid sliding up every single pane; climbing, climbing.

There was a tiny sound, high up, the *tink* of cracking glass. Then another, and another. *Tink-tink-tink* … the splintering came from every side as the small windows began to give way.

'What's happening?' asked Graham apprehensively.

'Too dark to see all the way up there,' said Ryan, squinting. He sniffed. 'What's that, though? That smell. Sort of … metallic. Reminds me of …'

'Blood,' said Graham. 'It smells like blood.'

They looked at each other. Then, in unison, their gazes returned to the darkness above and the oncoming horror.

The figure of Pauline Einstein swelled as she approached, swallowing up the other two ghostly figures, absorbing them into her, thickening and growing with each step. Her face was a grotesque approximation of humanity; its distorted features pulled into a pleading expression. Her voice was an unpleasant whine. '*Come home, Alberrrt.*' Yaz clapped her hands over her ears. '*Come home and marry a nice simple girl … this one is not worthy of you … she is so … unmusical …*'

Mileva stepped in front of the apparition, ignoring the Doctor's warning shout. 'You shall not have him back!' she shouted up. 'We are to be happy, you hear me? Leave him alone!'

The giant head turned towards her and the eyes blazed dark fire. '*You and your bastard child …*' it hissed.

Mileva rocked on her feet, shocked. 'Do not call her that,' she said, but her voice was weakening. 'Her name is Lieserl! And she was no one's fault!'

'*Liar!*' the apparition roared.

Blood poured over the windowsill and began to stream across the floor. Yaz leapt back, away from the box of starfish. 'Doctor! Doctor, do something!'

'Albert!' The Doctor ran to Einstein, cowering against the wall. 'Albert, you can stop this! You have to fight back!'

'No,' said Albert, his hands over his face. 'No, no, no, no.'

'What do you love most in the world?' the Doctor persisted. 'Is it your work? Or is it that magnificent woman over there, fighting for *you*, willing to give up her life for *you*? The woman you want to marry, the one who's proved she's worth it, over and over? Are you going to let her die because of you, Albert? *Are you?*'

On the other side of the room, the apparition became a swelling, billowing mass of dark anger, enveloping Mileva within it. She screamed.

Einstein's head jerked up at the sound. He still looked terrified, but now the light in his eyes burned steadily.

He stood up.

The blood oozed its painfully slow way down the inside of the cathedral walls, visible as a dark sticky fluid as it reached the edge of the pools of light cast by the thick candles. More and more of it poured in at the top of the windows every minute. Those families who still occupied spaces near the outer walls hurried inwards, to the already packed mass of people. Terror grew. Whispers and stifled cries as people tripped and fell on each other filtered through the air. Candles flickered and died, and darkness closed in.

'Graham.' It was Marthe, close by. 'Listen. Johanna is breathing again. I don't know how or why, but … listen.'

Graham bent down. She was right. Johanna's breath was no longer catching in her throat. And although it was hard to tell in the dim light, her lips looked a little less blue.

'Do you think ...?' Marthe hardly dared finish the question.

Graham squeezed her hand. 'I told you not to give up hope.'

His reassuring smile faded as he turned to see the thick sticky liquid start to pool on the floor.

Yaz, pressed into a corner as the blood covered more and more of the floor, watched Einstein walk across to the whirling maelstrom that surrounded Mileva and reach into it. The smoke drew back from him, as if his touch were toxic. In the cloud, the face of Pauline Einstein could still be seen, twisted with anger.

Mileva choked, 'Albert?'

'It's me,' he said. 'Help me.'

'Yes!' she said. 'Of course, yes, yes! Always.'

He took both her hands. Above them, the apparition hesitated. The blood too held back its boiling advance.

'Go on, Albert,' the Doctor urged him. 'Talk to Mileva. About the two of you.'

'Dollie,' said Einstein. 'My darling Dollie. All this time, we have battled together, haven't we? Even when I thought you didn't love me, and you thought I didn't love you.'

Mileva gave a little laugh. 'So many letters of apology from my sweet Johnnie.'

'She is a bad choice,' the voice of Pauline whined.

Albert shook his head, not taking his eyes from Mileva for a moment. 'No,' he said, 'she is the best choice

I could make. She understands me like no one else. Like you never did.'

The apparition's mouth opened in horror, but no sound came out. Smoke began to evaporate from its limbs.

'The only girl in the class.' Albert smiled warmly at Mileva. 'How lucky I was! To find someone with such a brilliant mind to work alongside, and then to find there was more than that.'

Tears sprang to Mileva's eyes. 'So much more.'

'The ghosts are shrinking!' the Doctor called. 'You're doing it, Albert!'

Yaz breathed a shaky sigh of relief as the blood receded across the floor, thinning and evaporating. The apparition above them broke into pieces that flared briefly and burned out like ash from a bonfire.

'I'm so sorry.' Albert kissed his sweetheart's hands. 'I've caused you so much pain and worry. And I've put you in such danger. But you never gave up on me.'

'I never would,' said Mileva softly.

Albert stepped forward and pulled her close to him. The final fragments of the ghostly mother vanished into the air, and the floor was clean again.

The tide of blood had reached the floor of the cathedral, but now, for the first time, it had slowed.

'What's it waiting for?' Ryan murmured.

As they watched, the liquid thinned and became blurry, like mist on a mirror. Ryan rubbed his eyes. 'Is it – disappearing?'

Within seconds, it was as though the blood had never been. Relief swept through the congregation.

And Johanna opened her eyes.

Back in the Rathaus, silence hung thickly until the Doctor strode over to the couple and said, 'Albert, that was some serious strength of character there. You've done the hard bit, but we've still got to draw in all these starfish.'

Einstein looked baffled. 'What?'

'I know what to do.' Mileva wiped her eyes. 'Come with me, darling. It's going to take both of us. I'm not letting you do it on your own again.' She picked up the embellished saucepan and placed it on her own head. 'It's not a very elegant bonnet.' Then she took Albert's hands in hers. 'We're going to imagine. Imagination's what the starfish need, isn't it, Doctor?'

'That's right.'

'There's something Albert and I imagined for a long time ... What our life might have been like ... with Lieserl, the baby we had last year.' Mileva's voice trembled. She took a breath and said more firmly, 'Albert, imagine with me. Imagine Lieserl, the daughter they made us give away. Imagine what she is doing now.'

Albert said, 'She is sleeping.'

'Yes. What is her room like? The room we have never seen, in the home of the people we have never met.'

'It is ... white. With green curtains and a white dresser.'

'Yes,' agreed Mileva. 'And she sleeps in a white cot that hangs from a cradle. It rocks her asleep.'

'When she wakes,' Albert said, 'she will go out in her pram ...'

The Doctor pulled on Yaz's arm. 'Time to get back to work. I'm going to send the ultraviolet beam through the amplifier.' She twisted a setting on the sonic and plugged it back into the machine. Instantly, the whole sky was alight with floating stars. Yaz and the Doctor began to pluck the feather-light creatures out of the air and thrust them into the tea chest as fast as they could.

'Before long, she will be taking her first steps,' Mileva was saying.

'Early,' said Albert. 'She is our child – she will be early to do everything. Clever, a little scientist.'

'Going on adventures. Pond-dipping. Splashing in puddles. Riding a bicycle.'

'I see her wearing a red dress,' Albert said.

'With yellow daisies,' Mileva continued.

'And matching red shoes.'

'With white socks.'

'Doctor,' said Yaz, trying to squash down the creatures inside the tea chest, 'we need another box.' Above Albert and Mileva, a new cloud started to swirl into being. 'Doctor, it's happening again! He's losing it!'

'No,' the Doctor said, a grin spreading over her face. 'Look. It's not made of smoke. It's made of light.' Indeed, the cloud that was forming over the couple's heads was bright white, flashes of silver darting in and out.

'One day,' said Albert to Mileva, 'we will see her again …'

And the cloud of light took shape, a figure in a dress and socks and shoes, holding a bunch of wildflowers and laughing.

'It's her,' said Yaz. 'It's Lieserl.'

Mileva and Albert looked up too, and Mileva whispered, 'My little girl.'

'*Our* little girl,' countered Albert. 'The brightest star in the universe.'

Lieserl smiled down at Albert and Mileva and released her flowers, which turned into a shower of petals. Then she held out her arms, and the starfish flowed towards her like a river. She folded them into her arms, her pockets, into her hair and dress, until her whole being was illuminated with them.

'Their minds are creating the solution,' the Doctor said softly to Yaz. 'Incredible.'

In the cathedral, a hush fell over the crowd as every single person looked up at the stars of light that had appeared way up in the ceiling. 'What are they?' breathed Ryan.

Graham shook his head, wonderingly. 'It's like something out of Disney.'

'Look at the pretty lights, Mama,' said Johanna as the glowing stars began to drift out through the broken windows. Friedrich hugged her to him as Marthe burst into happy tears.

'Come on,' Ryan said to Graham, 'outside!' He led the way over to the nearest door, pushing past the awestruck police officer and unbarring it. 'Wow.'

Münsterplatz was illuminated by thousands of floating lights streaming overhead, driven by invisible currents. Lights flowed from windows, from roofs, from towers and pavements as the first rays of dawn painted thin stripes across the sky.

'Grace would've loved this,' said Graham quietly.

More and more people came out, curious to see the sight. And, as the river of stars flowed by, more and more children inside the cathedral opened their eyes.

When Lieserl had tucked the very last starfish into her hair, she smiled down again and waved to her parents. Then she took a little breath and shrank to the size of a flower, which floated down into the box of starfish. Yaz fitted the lid, and there was silence.

The Doctor, inevitably, broke it. 'Nicely done, you two. Sorry about your gramophone, by the way. And your forks. Still, who needs forks, eh?'

Mileva smiled at her. 'Forks can be replaced. Hearts and minds cannot.'

'You know ...' Albert looked around the room, taking in the high ceilings and the tall windows in the early morning light. 'This would be the perfect place to be married.'

'Here?' said Yaz.

'Why not? It's not Jewish, nor Catholic – if we marry here, we can annoy *both* sets of parents.' Einstein grinned impishly at Mileva, who laughed.

A familiar wheezing sound reached their ears. Yaz dashed to the window. 'It can't be!'

Down in the street outside stood a familiar blue box. 'Doctor, why is the TARDIS here?'

'It's a younger TARDIS,' said the Doctor, looking slightly embarrassed. 'We're going to have to run, Yaz. Remember I said I mustn't bump into myself? Looks like I've just arrived.' She turned to Mileva and Albert. 'So sorry we can't stay. But don't worry – you're in *very* good hands, I promise. Just don't tell him a thing about any of this.' She winked. 'You're fairly good at making things up ... C'mon, Yaz, grab the other handle of this box.'

Yaz gave Mileva a hug, and shook Albert's hand. 'It was amazing to meet you both,' she said. 'I think you're going to have a fantastic wedding.'

Between them, the Doctor and Yaz carried the tea chest to the top of the exterior staircases. Someone with a shock of curly brown hair was making his way up. 'Down the other side!' hissed the Doctor urgently. 'Ah!' they heard a booming voice say as the figure reached the top. 'Good, I'm glad there's someone here. I heard there's been some unusual goings-on ...'

'Nothing for *you* to worry about,' said the Doctor under her breath, as she and Yaz ducked out of the building and onto the Rathausplatz. 'Never mind. We'll miss the wedding – but I miss Ryan and Graham more!'

The crowds in Münsterplatz were bathed in pale dawn light by the time Yaz and the Doctor arrived. 'It's about time,' said Graham, coming to meet them. 'We've had all sorts here – rats, comas, blood, floating stars.'

'Really?' said the Doctor. 'That sounds very exciting.'

'What's in the box?' asked Ryan.

'Floating stars,' said Yaz.

'Ask a silly question,' said Graham.

'Those light things,' said Ryan, 'is that where they went?'

'With a bit of encouragement,' the Doctor agreed. 'Everyone here is all right now, then?'

'Yep,' said Graham. 'All the kids are awake, and they're hungry, so I reckon they're fine.'

The Doctor nodded, satisfied. 'They're not the only ones. I know this little diner on Fantabulax II. Does the *best* cheeseburgers. We just need to make a quick stop first to drop off these little fellas somewhere they can't do any damage.' She patted the box. 'Pretty things, weigh almost nothing, nearly destroyed a city. Never judge a book by its cover.' Graham and Ryan took hold of the box, and the four friends started threading their way through the square back to the park.

'Wait a minute,' said Graham. 'What about Einstein? Did you get to see him?'

'Oh yeah,' said the Doctor. 'Bless him and his bonkersly marvellous brain.'

'Can't we meet him?' asked Ryan. 'I thought that was the whole point of coming here.'

'Think the TARDIS had her own ideas about that,' the Doctor said.

'Glad we could sort things out,' said Yaz as they reached their TARDIS. 'No more ghostly nightmares.'

'Oh, there'll always be nightmares.' The Doctor opened the door and ushered in her friends. 'You can't get rid of them; they'll always be popping up in one form or another. But the thing about dreams is – the good ones are always stronger than the bad.'

The door clicked shut.

Who-Dini?

Steve Cole

It's the travel that's the greatest. Seventeen years old and I've seen more states and stages than some dancing girls see in a lifetime. Chicago, right now and for eight weeks, the brand new Uptown theatre: fancy as a palace but even better with those amazing neon hoardings outside, singing its name from North Side clear across the city.

There's four thousand seats inside, and each and every one is taken each and every night: people watching and gasping and paying up to a dollar-fifty a ticket as the great Harry Houdini ties me up and turns me into a butterfly, or conjures me out of the giant radio in my glittering outfit. It's like I'm living in a dream. Mr and Mrs H have taken small-time Dorothy Smith and treated her like their big-time daughter. They couldn't have kids themselves, I heard, but to them, me and Judy and the other six new assistants, and their prop guys of course, we're all one big family.

Course, every family has secrets. The Houdinis depend on them, thrive on them, live them day and night. And because Mr and Mrs H are magical folk, so are their secrets. We drag them in crates across the country in a 60-foot railway car, to only the finest places, and what's real, what isn't, it all kind of melts and makes something new.

In Baltimore, not long after we opened, I walked in on Mrs H in the dressing room, and she was at the back looking into this big table mirror. Only it wouldn't show my reflection, like I wasn't really there. And I saw that Mrs H's face was young again, no more than my age, just gazing back at her.

'Leave me, Dorothy,' Mrs H murmured like she was half asleep. Only then did the reflection catch up and mouth the words. Well, I was scared; I turned round and left and walked round in a daze. Later on, I got up nerve to sneak back when the dressing room was empty and I saw there wasn't even any glass in that mirror. It was just air and empty.

Yesterday I saw her in Houdini's arms backstage. Only, I'd just brought a coffee to Houdini in the star dressing room where he was resting up ahead of his performance – he'd been out all day – so who the heck was this? Course, Houdini does a new illusion in this show, where he seems to get killed in a locked cabinet on the stage and then thirty seconds later he bursts out at the back of the auditorium, swinging on a trapeze. It brings down the house at the close of the second act. Only he can't wish himself through empty space, so ...

There's got to be an impersonator, right?

I said so yesterday to Billy, one of the new male assistants brought in by Mr Collins. Billy's in his twenties and he has the dreamiest eyes, like the best blue marbles. 'I reckon as how you're right,' he said, 'gotta be an impersonator,' but he had a smile on his face like he knew better.

It's a real good double, for sure. When he lands on the stage, holding up his arms, he looks just like the real deal, and sounds just like him too when he thanks the audience. Maybe he kisses Mrs H just like him?

It's like he knew what I was thinking, this man, cos he turned and looked at me, startled, and you couldn't mistake those eyes, the stare, the commanding air. I mean, it *was* Houdini.

Only now – somehow – he looked just the age he'd have been when he and Mrs H first met.

I didn't say anything, I just turned and left. I didn't even know where I was going. I wanted to find Billy, to tell him what I'd seen – that I was right, it *was* an impersonator, and now he was impersonating with Mrs H. But Billy was nowhere to be found, and in the end I found myself outside the door of the older Houdini in his star dressing room and I felt so bad for him, but I thought, I can't tell him. Because I didn't want to rock this lovely boat I'd wound up in.

I knocked, and the door was yanked open by Houdini. He was on the telephone and looked real worked up. When he spoke on stage, he made sure to sound clear and precise, like a stern professor reading aloud from a textbook. Now the accented voice was hot with rage: 'I haven't taken a damn thing from you, Gladstone. I was in the theatre all day yesterday and have witnesses who will swear to it. And believe me, had I wanted to get into this lock-up of yours, I would have!' Houdini slammed down the receiver and then he looked ready to do the same to me: 'What is it, Dorothy?'

I had not seen him so angry before. 'Are you, uh, OK, Mr Houdini?'

'That old fool Gladstone and his insinuations.' He was twisting at the big old ring he wore on his index finger. 'All these years and still these hacks and has-beens paw at my reputation. Always trying to tear me down to their level so my pockets are easier to pick.'

'You're top of the tree, sir,' I said.

'Of course I am.' He sat down on the bed, weary. 'There is no contrivance on Earth from which the Great Houdini cannot free himself, isn't that so?'

'The whole world knows that.'

'When you are older, my dear, you will come to realise that there are some things from which no one can escape. Not even the Great Houdini.'

His piercing eyes, as he looked at me, were exactly those of his double's.

I didn't know what to say. I made my excuses and left, hurried back through the dark warren that threaded the theatre's innards like veins. I was scared I'd run into Houdini's impostor again, but in fact I ran into Mrs H. She was alone on the stage and she stood, still as a mannequin, surrounded by the outsized props from the act that Mr Collins made. It looked kind of like they were ganging up on her.

Billy stepped up beside me, made me jump. 'You look like you saw a ghost,' he said.

'I saw Houdini's double from the act,' I whispered.

His eyes widened. 'You did?'

'And Mrs H and him, they were … well. I *think* that they were …'

Billy smiled. 'Working on a grand new finish for the show?'

I blinked. Was that what I'd seen? It could've been. Just part of an act, and all innocent. If I'd gone blabbing to Mr H …

'You ever get homesick, Dorothy?' Billy asked suddenly.

'Are you kidding?' I shook my head. 'There's so much to do and see.'

'Some day, I reckon you will,' he said. 'The places where you grew, the people you knew – that helped make you what you are.'

I kept my eyes on Mrs H so he couldn't see me blush when I said to him, 'What about the people you're going to get to know – the ones who might make you better?'

'You get tired of looking,' said Billy. 'When do you stop? In the end you have to settle someplace. Look at Mrs H – she's settled for a stage.'

I watched Mrs H as she put her hand to the wide wooden sides of the big Radio of 1950, the same prop I jumped out of each night doing the Charleston; the job she'd have done twenty years ago.

'Guess a stage can be any place,' I said. I looked round, but Billy had gone.

I wanted to keep talking. But I guess I'll get my chance. We're on tour for 36 weeks, 8 of them here in Chicago. I'm a part of a big success story, magical in every way, and the Hs are such good people.

It's just not fair that this awful mood's come over them both. The morning papers were full of this awful business they're calling The Magician Murders. Two old-time stage illusionists dead so far. Mr H knew them both a long time back; old duffers, he called them. And he says he's not worried, that he'll stay safe.

Now another old friend of his has showed. The Doctor. He looks like he might be a magician too.

And he looks the exact opposite of safe.

'The Magician Murders!' The Doctor threw back his latest head and laughed, the roar echoing off the dark tenements along the Chicago River. 'You'll be safe then, Harry. You're not a magician, you're a Supreme Ruler of Mystery– wasn't that what you used to put on the playbills?'

Houdini glared across at his old friend, and quickly regretted it. No one could out-stare the Doctor while he wore this form: a mighty voltage blazed in those stone-hard eyes, locked beneath the Victorian preacher brows. This Doctor's soul matched his dress: austere and dark but with rich flashes of colour, a right companion with whom to venture into cold and moonlit danger.

'The first man to die,' said Houdini, 'was Dean Kellar, "The Dean D'Illusion".'

'Terrible title.'

'Terrible act,' Houdini snorted. 'Or used to be. These past few years his Third Eye trick has drawn bill-topping business.'

'And so perhaps marked him out for murder along with …' The Doctor consulted the *Tribune*'s front page article. 'The Miracle-Monger, Gregor Yarinski?'

'Yarinski was a relic until he spruced up his act with a bulletproof cage—'

'Miracle-Monger?' The Doctor looked nauseated. 'All right, all right, so what am I doing here – your bodyguard?'

'I have not asked for your assistance because I fear attack.'

'Why, then?' The Doctor's grey hair was ruffled in the wind blowing in across the river. 'Why come to the scene of the latest crime on your one night off in weeks?'

Houdini hesitated. Then he nodded ahead to a large, shadowy redbrick edifice beside the rotting docks, far from the nearest streetlamps. 'Gladstone insists I was seen at his lock-up around the time Yarinski's murder took place. He threatens to go to the press.'

'But you weren't there?'

'Naturally not.'

'Then why accuse you?'

'Envy? Resentment?' Houdini spoke carefully; the Doctor was as good at scenting lies as selling them, they had that much in common. 'Like the Dean and Yarinski, Gladstone is an elder of the Magicians' Innermost Circle, and a spiritualist medium to boot. Such charlatans do not enjoy the way I expose their tricks and hokum.'

The Doctor looked over to the warehouse. 'What's kept in there?'

'I had no idea until Gladstone gave it away,' said Houdini. 'It seems that he and Yarinski have pooled their resources over the years and have gathered a vast, secret collection of magic props and paraphernalia, dating back centuries.'

'Then, we're here to gather evidence so Houdini can solve the murder, clear his name, win the freedom of the city and put still more bums on seats?' The Doctor gave him a studied look. 'Definitely not to steal secrets ...'

'I already have secrets enough for two lifetimes.'

'And I have lifetimes enough to learn them all.'

They walked on, and Houdini said nothing more. The waterfront was haunted only by the throb of distant traffic, the whole bank of the river deserted. Outside Gladstone's warehouse, a length of rope strung between sawhorses was the only sign of any police investigation. Houdini led the way cautiously to a side door and looked expectantly at the Doctor who produced his sonic screwdriver.

'Ah! Your magician's wand still works, even after our adventures underwater?' Houdini observed, remembering the last time their paths had crossed in New England – or rather splashed, when recovering the body of a sea monster from the bottom of Gloucester Harbor. 'You still refuse to sell it to me?'

'Patent pending.' The Doctor held his sonic to the lock and the door creaked open onto must and darkness. 'Setting 211 – energetic excitation of the oxygen atoms to generate light.' The sonic whirred, a prickling red glow above them lit the warehouse, and the Doctor smiled at Houdini. 'Could've just used the light on the end as a torch, of course, but where's the fun in that?'

Houdini spared only moments to appreciate the marvel of the conjured light, distracted by the array of tea chests and packing cases, scattered with reams of dusty playbills and posters like ancient scrolls.

The Doctor stared accusingly at the shadows. In one of them a tall crate had been torn open, the wood lying in splintered planks, and the Doctor waved his screwdriver over the smooth curves of white metal within, which reached to roughly half the height of the box. 'Well, this is very interesting.'

'It's the lower section of Yarinski's bulletproof cabinet,' Houdini murmured. 'He would stand inside and invite shooting parties to open fire. No bullets of any kind ever marked it.'

'With atmospheric shielding of this kind, I'm not surprised.' The Doctor kicked it lightly, and a green sheen glimmered about the metal. 'It's the lower section of the psycho-shell of a macro-kinetic transport pod. A device for traversing the stars – reduced by ignorance to a stage prop.'

'A ship to the stars, you say?' Houdini marvelled. 'If I'd only known . . .'

'You couldn't have, I'm glad to say.' The Doctor flashed a mirthless smile, put on a pair of thick dark spectacles, and turned back to the metal curves. 'This is the only thing broken into, so the pod must be what the murderer wanted. But it seems both segments were here for the taking, so why run away with the piloting system and leave the drive behind . . .?'

Houdini felt the hairs on the back of his neck prickle – a familiar feeling – and held a hand up to the

Doctor, bidding him be silent as he peered all around. 'Come out!' he pointed to the shadows dramatically. 'Show yourself!'

A short, stooped old man in a brown suit stepped out from behind an Egyptian sarcophagus. He leaned on a silver-topped cane the way his bulbous nose rested on a scrubbing brush moustache. In his left hand he held a gun.

Houdini simply inclined his head stiffly. 'Gladstone.'

'Well!' Gladstone had the smile of a starved cat. 'Intruders, have I? And one so eminent as Harry Houdini! Had a feeling you'd come looking once I'd baited the trap.'

'That was why you telephoned, then? As a lure?'

'And you couldn't resist. I *knew* you'd be here.'

'Because you used your Third Eye?' The Doctor tweaked the sonic and something like a glowing ball bearing fell from the rafters and bounced on the floor. 'Or in other words, the camera-drone designed to monitor the occupant of this travel pod. Very handy for identifying the contents of a lady's handbag in your act, I'm sure – or for making sure your intended victim is on his way so you can make your big entrance.'

Gladstone looked shaken for a moment. Then he stared at the little sphere and it buzzed back up into the rafters. 'These murders are a distressing business, but why not turn it to one's advantage?' He licked his lips and seemed to find them appetising. 'I have caught the two of you red-handed, trespassing on my property. You attack me, I shoot you in self-defence. Think of the disgrace when the police arrive – the ageing Houdini, as tired and uninspired as his act, so desperate for fresh magical secrets that he would steal for them!'

The Doctor cleared his throat impatiently. 'The real story here is, what's an alien space travel system doing boxed up in a Chicago warehouse? Where did you get this?'

'One of many items from P. T. Barnum's personal Collection of Otherworldly Wonder,' Gladstone revealed.

'Poppycock!' Houdini made each syllable a pistol shot. 'You never dealt with Barnum.'

'Wiseman King did the deal – the Prince of the Preternatural!' Gladstone nodded. 'When he retired following that unfortunate bit of business with the showgirls, he was persuaded to make a sale or two, wasn't he? As well you know, Harry.'

'And he sold this to Yarinski.' The Doctor's lip had curled. 'Well, what else to do with a travel pod that can't travel? Not with this slave restraint relay built into its workings.'

Gladstone raised a mocking eyebrow. 'You claim to understand this?'

'The craft was designed to dispatch a slave creature to its new owner. That owner must have possessed a restraint control of some sort to punish it if it disobeyed; there's a secondary circuit built into the drive system here to stop the creature from using this craft to escape. At least –' The Doctor pressed the side of his glasses and smiled – 'until I destroy that relay.'

A fierce flash of light jumped from the base of the craft in a cloud of purple smoke. Gladstone reeled back – as Houdini lunged forward, snatched the gun and covered him in turn. 'Ha! You performed the Bullet Catch trick in your young day, Gladstone, did you not? Let us not test what you remember of it.'

Gladstone opened his mouth to retort – and a spiked claw burst out from inside, like a horrible tongue, as it skewered the back of his skull.

'No!' The Doctor shouted.

The creature behind Gladstone was a huge, albino biped festooned with twitching claws and jaws like some monstrous Venus flytrap. Over its head and torso it wore an arrangement of opaque glass and metal – clearly the second, piloting piece of the travel pod. As Gladstone's corpse thudded to the floor, the creature let out a threatening shriek that the glass helmet did little to muffle.

'Stay back!' Houdini raised the gun as the Doctor bawled the same thing, only to Houdini. But the creature barged past them both and leapt into the metal pod. It glowed a deep beetroot colour, huffing and steaming until, in a magnesium flash, it was gone..

'Fast worker, wasn't he?' The Doctor got up and dusted himself down. He looked disgusted – most likely with himself. 'I don't recognise the species, but had I known it was hiding here, I clearly wouldn't have burned out the restraint system ...'

'It must have been after Gladstone.' Houdini was on his knees, glaring at the old man's body; in the brown suit he looked like a stubbed out cigar. 'What have you done?'

'Set it free. Free to escape through space at the speed of thought; it'll be the other side of the solar system by now.'

'What have you done?' Houdini said again, closing his eyes. 'What have you done …?'

I was at the stage door that night, tasting the air when the Great Houdini and the Doctor came back. Bess – Mrs H – was working late in the theatre costume shop sewing extra sequins to our costumes. I could've taken a cab back to the brownstone off Michigan Avenue where we were staying, but I promised my mom and dad I would never be out of the company of either Mr or Mrs Houdini, and with Mr H out of the way that night …

As soon as I'd opened the door I'd seen the police box standing there in the alley. It hadn't been there the night before. Houdini was making for it now with the Doctor, and they both looked real serious.

'You're sure it's gone?' Houdini said.

'It's far, far from here. Don't worry, no one will know we were at Gladstone's.' He tossed something like a ball bearing in his palm then pushed it into his pocket.

They shook hands, and – get this – the Doctor walked inside the police box and the light started flashing, and this wind started up with the strangest sound, and litter was blowing all around. Mr H's hair was standing up, and the police box was just fading away. *It's just an illusion, Dorothy,* I told myself, though my eyes were hanging on stalks. *It's just what the boss does.*

'What have you done?' Houdini shouted to the air, and he sounded so anguished. As the last bits of the blue box took off into the night he hung his head.

But even as the sound faded it started up again, and so did the gale, only this time behind Houdini. I looked and couldn't believe it. The box was coming back! It didn't look just exactly the same but near enough. Houdini looked real startled as he turned to face it and, as the edges hardened and the wind dropped, a figure burst out from inside. It was a woman, with blonde hair and soft features; she charged up to Houdini, grinning, and just from her being there the alley seemed warmer by a couple of degrees.

'Harry!' She put her hands on his shoulders. 'Harry, what I told you, I was wrong. That creature in the warehouse – it hasn't left Earth! I doubt if it's even left Chicago!'

Houdini stared at her.

'It hit me, not five minutes ago. I was reminiscing with my gang, telling them about the good times, like that sea monster in Gloucester Harbor. How wet did we get, eh? And those chains the hunters clapped us in!' She clapped his cheeks with both hands as if to demonstrate. 'Oh, sorry, Harry, I forgot. It's me. Still me – the Doctor!'

'You are a woman now?' Houdini said at last.

'Probably, yeah. Well, you've done it too! Remember that illusion you used to do with Bess – Metamorphosis! You go in the crate and she's your assistant and then you come out and she's in the crate and you're *her* assistant ...?' She beamed and waved to the police box behind her. 'Well, that's my crate! Anyway, listen, that thing at Gladstone's lock-up. It can't have gone far.'

'How can you know this—?' Houdini began.

'It just struck me, BAM!' She slapped a hand to her forehead. 'Remember I excited the oxygen molecules with the sonic? Showing off. Lit the place red. BUT! I just realised, macro-kinetic transmission energies on anything more than a local hop would've *super*-excited those oxygen molecules, put us in the dark. But that didn't happen, and so, question is – whereabouts in the neighbourhood did that creature go?'

I had no idea what she was talking about. I had even less idea why Houdini would suddenly look so relieved.

He looked at her. 'You believe the creature is still close by?'

'Yeah. I do. Unfinished business. The Magician Murders may not be over.' The Doctor looked haunted. 'That's why I'm back here! I set that creature free but it hasn't gone – and it mustn't be allowed to kill again. But how do we find it, eh ...?'

I stopped listening as I saw three more people coming out from the blue box, a dark-skinned boy and girl not much older than me, and a man as old as my daddy. And I felt bad for thinking it, but that was a better illusion than I ever saw Houdini do. They weren't parading for applause, though, just looking around in wonder. Like they'd never been in a Chicago back-alley before.

'Ryan! Yaz! Graham!' The Doctor threw open her arms. 'Come and meet the great Harry Houdini!'

I slipped back inside, just then, into the gloomy corridor, and of course it was the perfect time to run into Billy coming around the corner with Mrs H.

'Dorothy!' she looked surprised. 'What are you doing here?'

'I was at the stage door,' I said. 'Mr H is back with the Doctor ... only the Doctor's different.'

'Ah, that old trick,' Mrs H said fondly. 'He can change his physical appearance. He does it a lot.'

'He is a she!'

Mrs H just laughed. 'Is she now!'

Billy looked at Mrs H. 'Sounds quite a talent, changing appearance like that. I'd like to meet … her.'

Mrs H met his smiling eyes and nodded. 'I think we all would.'

The Doctor and her group had no digs so Houdini put everyone up at the townhouse. That meant that me and Julie had to share our room with Yaz. No problem – what a Sheba! She looks like an Indian princess, even if she dresses like a boy. Ryan, on the other hand, is the most beautiful boy I've ever seen, though he smells like a girl; he shared the basement with the stagehands. Graham slept on the floor in Mr Collins' room. They both love their bosses, sure, but I bet they had fun complaining about all the looking out for them that they do. The Doctor refused the Houdinis' bed and took the tub. Maybe she was a man yesterday, or maybe not – maybe I don't get it but, either way, she's a real bearcat. The whole bunch of us mucked in and got along. I love that in a company, you know? When you just have the feeling that things are fine.

Next morning we all had breakfast at the big and busy table, all together. Houdini looked kind of tired, like he hadn't slept. The morning paper was folded in front of him, and its leader yelled out the murder of another magician, this one called Mr Gladstone. I felt kind of scared at the idea of a third Magician Murder, but Mr Collins tried to laugh it off: 'These acts have been dying on stage for years. And there are so many magicians in Vaudeville it'll take 'em years to get round to Houdini ...'

The big man himself put down his grapefruit fork and changed the subject for us. 'Your blue police box is crowded these days, Doctor.' He gave an expansive wave at Yaz, Ryan and Graham, then favoured me with a smile. 'I, too, change my assistants regularly. Beauty, strength and the reassurance of experience – these are what we master mystifiers demand, eh, Doctor!'

The Doctor looked at her friends, speechless for a moment. Then she just laughed.

'Well, fair play, I'm beauty,' Graham deadpanned.

'Strength,' Yaz said at once, grinning.

'And I'm just *so* reassuringly experienced,' said Ryan, shaking his head.

I giggled and wondered if Billy had noticed how much I looked at Ryan, but no; he was staring out the window, his food untouched.

The Doctor pulled something strange from her pocket, like a stick of pewter with a crystal on the end. 'Well, lovely as it is to eat grapefruits in the morning – what a brilliant idea, who thought that up? I should thank them – we have stuff to do.'

Houdini reached out casually. 'Your sonic screwdriver has changed ...'

'But you haven't.' She slapped his fingers away, and Mrs H laughed out loud. 'It might be a long shot ... but I'm gonna scan.'

'Scan for what, Doctor?' Yaz said.

'Technology relating to the creature that killed Yarinski all that time ago – um, yesterday.' She was studying her metal stick. 'Our visitor got away in a macro-kinetic transmission pod, and tech like that leaves a very distinctive disturbance in the local atmosphere. So if he's still about the Chicago area I ought to be able to . . .' The stick started to thrum and the crystal glowed faintly. 'To pick him up! Ha, there we are!'

'Where?' Billy looked at her, rose from his chair. 'Tell me where—'

'Mind your place, lad,' Houdini snapped. 'Sit down.' And Billy sat.

'Ooh!' The stick's crystal glowed a deep red, enthralling the Doctor. 'Power surge! There's tech operating right now, and it's close.'

Graham looked alarmed. 'What, here in the house, you mean?'

'Hard to say exactly.' The Doctor shrugged. 'Maybe.'

I was first on my feet, though Julie and Mr Collins were close behind me.

'Everyone needs to stay calm,' Yaz said.

'Nobody's gonna get hurt,' Ryan promised.

'This creature murders magicians, after all,' said Mrs H. 'It will have no taste for anyone else.'

'So it's Houdini and the Doctor we've got to worry about,' Yaz reasoned.

'It could have killed us yesterday if it had wanted to,' the Doctor said. 'Just like it killed poor old Gladstone.'

'Bumping you off could still be on its to-do list!' said Graham. 'What do we do, Doc, evacuate?'

'Lock ourselves in the basement!' I suggested.

'Never back yourself into someplace there's no other way out of,' the Doctor said, and Houdini joined in as she added, 'First rule of escaping.' She was waving her pewter stick around like a magic wand. 'All right, everyone. The surge has died down. No immediate danger – but it's still about.'

'Comforting,' said Graham.

I reached for Billy's hand without thinking, and he squeezed my fingers. I saw Mrs H was holding his other hand, to comfort *him.*

'It's no good! The sonic's not accurate enough to give me more.' She put the strange rod away in her pocket. 'I need bits and bobs from my police box to fix the reading.'

'In the alley by the theatre? I'll go with you,' Billy said. 'If you're a magician too, you'll be in danger.'

'Thanks,' said Graham, 'but we've got this, mate.'

'No one gets past Strength and Beauty,' Yaz added with a smile at Ryan. 'Wouldn't you agree, Reassuring Experience?'

'Bitter experience,' Ryan muttered.

'We must all accompany the Doctor,' Houdini spoke firmly. 'The Uptown will be a safer place to wait things out than here. I know the space; whatever comes, we will have the advantage.'

So Houdini's drivers took us to the theatre. While the Doctor disappeared into the blue box to magic herself up whatever she needed to find the magician murderer, her friends joined the rest of us backstage. There was still work to do: embellishing the costumes, testing the trick contraptions, making sure they worked as smooth as silk stockings. I watched Billy and the stagehands work under Mr Collins' direction in the shops: it would only take one failure, one little feature less than perfect, to wreck a perfect illusion.

Everything's so fragile, I thought. The gap between the trick and the truth so small.

'Dorothy?' Ryan came up beside me. 'Any chance of a guided tour upstairs?'

'Now?' I almost blushed. 'Just the two of us, you mean?'

'Yeah, it's all right. The Doctor just asked us to search for ... well, you know, any ways in and out this thing could use.' He smiled. 'Julie's showing Yaz around the trap room, workshops and the fly space, Graham is checking front of house and all round the outside. Thought we could look through the dressing rooms?'

'Sure,' I told him. I saw Billy look my way as we left, and he didn't look happy. I felt a flutter inside to see that look on his face.

'I can show you my dressing room,' I said as we headed upstairs. 'We all share it, me and Julie and the chorus girls. But Mr and Mrs H, they've got the star rooms, they're locked.'

'That's what these are for.' Ryan held up a bunch of keys. 'These are the masters from security.'

I stared. 'How'd you get those? You stole 'em?'

'I'm returning them! Think the Doctor borrowed them next year and never put them back.' He shrugged. 'We've got to look everywhere, right – to keep everyone safe?'

And I felt safe with Ryan, I did. I had to help him with the keys, he wasn't so good trying to turn all the different ones in the locks, but it was a real thrill, you know, checking out the Houdinis' private dressing rooms when they weren't there. Kind of like we were doing something wrong to do right. That's what it felt like.

Right up until we found this big glowing metal cabinet in two halves, sitting in Mrs H's wardrobe.

'Oh, my days,' Ryan said. 'The Doctor told me to watch for this. Think it's what that creature uses to travel.' He grabbed my arm and ran from the room, pulling me after him. 'Which means the thing must already be here in the theatre – come on!'

But on the landing we ran straight into two men with handguns. One of them smashed the butt of his pistol into the side of Ryan's head and he went down. I opened my mouth to scream and the other thug grinned and pointed his revolver in my face.

'Don't,' he said.

Houdini stood alone on the silent stage, staring out over the acre of seats before him. Behind him hung the vast tapestry Bess had spent weeks putting together from copies of all the medals and ribbons and certificates he'd received over the years, touring Europe and America, flying over Australia, dazzling the world. They hung now like mocking memories of youth. He and Bess had been so close, back then, reaching for the top together.

He forced himself to focus, pictured the sea of rapt faces that would be filling the theatre that evening and tried to remember the thrill he'd once taken from deceiving and delighting those ordinary people, the energy he'd thrived on that made life seem bright. These days everything felt greyer. His wrist throbbed as it so often did now, since breaking it twice in his movie days. His body ached. He'd ascended to the heights of his profession and he'd done so much to stay there. This show, three acts in one, had been running for months already, and already its innovations were being dismantled by the lesser types, the men like Gladstone and Yarinski who took magic and hid it in lock-ups to gloat over instead of bringing fresh wonders to the world. Houdini felt the pressure to push himself more keenly than ever, but was all too aware he'd be turning fifty-two in just a few weeks. And still the bookings, the challenges, the trains and the cars and commitments ...

Houdini could hold his breath longer than any man on Earth, but he still needed space enough to draw it now and again.

The Doctor's beautiful friend, Yaz, approached him, her tread soft, her eyes wide and dark. 'You all right?'

'All right?' Houdini meditated on this for a time, then smiled. 'The Doctor has asked you to watch over me ... Strength?'

'That's me,' Yaz agreed with a smile. 'And, you know, happy to. I mean, there's only one Harry Houdini. Your name lives on for ever.'

'The Great Houdini who can cheat fate?' Houdini smiled and flexed his tender wrist. 'The Doctor has shown you many things, I am sure. Many wonders, and many escapes. But there is something that no man can escape, and that is why the Doctor lives as he – as *she* – does.'

'What's that, then – old age? Death and taxes?'

'It is this world, my dear.' Houdini shook his head. 'The world we strive to create for ourselves, with its privileges, its luxuries and accolades. That is the velvet prison we fashion, and once we swing the door shut on ourselves we cannot leave it.'

'There's one way to escape it, the same way Gladstone did. And believe me, I've seen enough of that travelling with the Doctor too.' Yaz's face had hardened. 'You think she does what she does to escape your idea of prison? No way. She sees what's wrong and she can't turn away from it. She has to get involved, has to help. That's *her* prison.'

Houdini nodded thoughtfully. 'Perhaps you're right. I never met a less selfish soul. I wish I had learned from her example.'

'There's still time,' said Yaz simply. 'Choose a better way out. You can do that. You're Houdini.' She smiled. 'Speaking of which ... I know it's not the best time, but d'you think I could see some of your act?'

'Ha! As you wish it.' Houdini gave a small bow. 'Bess!' he called back to behind the curtain. 'Is Billy with you, perhaps? I wish to demonstrate to Yaz here our "Reincarnation".'

A few seconds later, Bess pushed through the curtain and, of course, Billy certainly was with her. The way she mothered him and how he in turn indulged her foolish fancies – it made Houdini's flesh creep.

'Reincarnation?' Bess flashed Yaz an awkward smile. 'We don't need to rehearse this again, Harry, do we? Considering what's happened ...'

Houdini returned the coolness of her gaze. 'Whatever … distractions we face now, I need to know that all will be perfect when I perform. Besides, how can we disappoint our eager audience?' He gestured to Yaz. 'The Doctor is not yet back with her machine to receive the signals of this … creature?'

'Not yet.'

'Well.' Houdini took a deep breath, let his measured stage voice boom across the auditorium. 'The Doctor is not alone in her ability to switch forms with another – this I *did* learn from her … and him, and him, and him …' He turned to Billy and tapped the ring on his index finger. 'Go.'

Billy glanced at Bess. 'You only have to ask, Mr H.'

'Collins!' Bess hollered backstage. 'We're doing Reincarnation …'

'This is awesome.' Yaz scrambled down from the stage beside the orchestra pit and sat in the front row, grinning. 'You're sure it's OK for me to watch?'

Houdini bowed again and crossed to a dark, lacquered cabinet placed centre-stage. Billy walked away through the seating to the back of the theatre. No hesitation, Houdini noted, very good: the lad would make his way to the one reserved box in the theatre, which would be held empty tonight as usual in readiness …

'Now! In the act of Reincarnation, my dear Yaz, I shall project myself across the theatre.' He looked to Bess, who was pulling the sabres from the back of the cabinet as she watched Billy exit the auditorium.

'Ordinarily, I would be handcuffed many times by members of the audience and placed in chains before entering the Cabinet of Endings.'

Bess flashed the first sabre around with lethal skill as Houdini stepped back into the box. 'Dorothy does this on the night,' she explained, as she pressed the door of the cabinet closed. 'No one wants to see the old frump in the spotlight.'

'Come on, Bess, you look amazing,' Yaz called.

In the paint-stinking darkness of the cabinet, Houdini braced his arms against the sides and raised his legs as Bess outside slammed the first sabre into the cabinet at calf height. Then he quickly ducked into a crouch as the next blade sliced through at what would've been stomach height, and delivered a theatrical, bloodcurdling scream. He opened the catch on the trapdoor, which swung down into the space beneath the stage, the noise hidden by the swish of the third sabre biting at chest height. Houdini dropped down quickly into the gloomy, five-watt under-stage. Moments later, as the fourth blade bit at neck height, he swung the door back up into place, and the thump gave the illusion of a severed head striking the floor.

The silence felt wrong; usually it was filled with the startled whisperings of the audience. 'Houdini is dead,' he muttered. 'Now, let Houdini take his place.'

Just then he felt cold metal press up to the back of his neck. He turned and saw two glints in the shadows: a grin and a gun.

He recognised the man at once: Wiseman King's loyal manservant, a tame thug named Dawson.

Dawson gripped Houdini's hand, peering at his index finger. 'Good. You got the ring.'

Houdini pulled away sharply, pretended to overbalance and fell to the floor.

'No tricks,' Dawson hissed. 'C'mon. Mr King wants to see you.'

Yaz was leaning forward in her chair as the illusion surely neared its climax. Bess had delivered the final sabre and now looked pantomime dismayed. She stared out at the imaginary audience as if about to ask for help – then gasped and pointed to the back of the auditorium.

Yaz whirled round to find a familiar figure launching itself from the VIP box balcony, catching at a trapeze that dropped down from the shadows of the vaulted roof. She clapped with delight. Somehow, here was Houdini! Grasping the trapeze, swinging forward, letting go and somersaulting … as another trapeze dropped down just in time for him to catch it.

Then Bess screamed. When Yaz swung back round to the stage she'd vanished, the curtain billowing behind her exit. Part of the act …?

Yaz heard a second shriek, this one above her. An inhuman, ululating sound. The flying Houdini overhead was blurring in mid air, changing shape even as she watched – becoming a monster, twisted and yellow, with muscular legs, a head like a bull and thick misshapen wings. Yaz stared in horror as the creature landed heavily on the stage. One wing struck the cabinet, knocking it apart and triggering the trapdoor beneath. The creature swung its horned head from side to side, flapping the charred gristle of its wings as it stomped towards the curtain and pulled it down with a sweep of its monstrous claws.

Though she was terrified, Yaz knew that Houdini had to be down beneath the trapdoor. She climbed quietly up onto the stage – but the creature swung round and spied her. Swearing under her breath, Yaz slithered down into the gloom, pulled her phone from her pocket and swiped up for the torch. At her feet was Houdini's gold ring. She picked it up and as she did, she saw letters written in the dust on the floorboards: *WK – PP*.

'Whoa! Hello!' The Doctor's voice sounded from above.

Yaz pushed her head back up through the trapdoor and saw the Doctor had come on stage, the enormous creature bearing down over her. She was clutching an improbable gadget that looked like corks and cutlery jammed into a carriage clock with an old retro *Simon Says* instead of a dial. 'Nice to know my tech works – I found you!'

'Doctor,' Yaz called, 'that thing's a shapeshifter, he looked like Houdini just now. But the real Houdini's not here, only his ring, and—'

'Yaz, Doctor!' Graham had burst into the auditorium and was rushing to join them. 'Get away from that thing!'

But the terrifying creature was changing again, shrinking into a smaller, bipedal figure with tousled dark hair and blue eyes. 'I guess this looks better to you?'

'Billy!' Graham looked dismayed. 'Aww, Billy, I thought you were a good kid. Don't tell me you're an evil monster!'

'There are many kinds of monster,' Billy retorted. He shimmered, becoming a taller, glistening white creature festooned with snapping ovoid jaws and claws. 'Monsters who would steal and kidnap. Monsters who would enslave and exploit.'

'And escaping slaves who would kill?' The Doctor looked sadly up at the monster before her. 'Yaz, Graham. This is what killed Gladstone last night – and the other magicians.'

'They all used me. Or the technology that kept me here.' The albino creature dwindled in size, becoming Billy once again. 'They prospered from my slavery.'

'But you're free now,' the Doctor said. 'You had your travel pod – once I'd burnt out the restraint circuit, you could've left this planet and all its unkindness. Why didn't you?' Her gadget gave an electronic chime and she looked across to where Graham was helping Yaz out from the trapdoor. 'What's that you've got?'

'Just Houdini's ring,' Yaz said. 'He dropped it for us to find, beside some initials in the dust.'

'It is not a ring. It is the command circuit.' Billy advanced slowly on Yaz, his hand outstretched. 'It limits my actions, forces me to obey—'

'Then stay back!' Yaz said, holding out the ring. Billy gasped with pain. 'Oh, God, sorry!' Yaz felt sick, lowered her hands. 'Please, stay back, Billy. I won't use this. I don't want to control you.'

'The slavers did. Barnum did. Wiseman King did. Houdini did. But the ring is old, as I am. It is finally losing power.' Billy grimaced, but resumed his advance. 'Enough for me to defy its control …'

'Uh-uh. Sorry.' Suddenly the Doctor was standing right in front of him, shielding Yaz and Graham, blocking Billy's way. 'So the battery's running low, is it? Control growing erratic, so you can resist enough to sneak away and kill? Take revenge on those who wronged you, is that it?'

'To secure my future I must deal with my past,' Billy told her.

'Wait a minute,' said Yaz. 'Did you say Wiseman King controlled you?'

'King purchased me and my pod from the carnival man, Barnum, along with other salvage from the slaver ship that brought me here.'

'Down there in the dust, it says "WK – PP".'

'Wiseman King,' the Doctor breathed. 'Also known as Prince of the Preternatural!'

'A prince and a king?' Yaz turned up her nose. 'There's some ego, right there.'

'You reckon it's King who grabbed Houdini?' Graham said to Billy.

Billy nodded. 'I changed form to attack because Bess was taken by one of his men. King has links to the mob – no shortage of hirelings.'

'Why would he take the risk of grabbing Houdini and Bess from here?' Yaz said.

Graham shrugged. 'I guess with everything in the papers about the Magician Murders …'

'He'll know he's a target,' the Doctor concluded.

'King was the final magician on my list,' Billy hissed. 'He paid in his prime for me: a shapeshifter, his to command. Made me do … so many things.'

'Until he had to sell off his best assets to buy his way out of trouble. And now I imagine he wants his command ring back as security against what's coming.' The Doctor took the slim gold band from Yaz. 'He doesn't know its power's on the wane. I could fix it, of course, get it working again. Stop you the hard way.' She handed it to Billy. 'But I won't. We can figure this out together, I know it. And I know Houdini's been using you, and I'm sorry. But he's an old friend and I have to help him now – and help him to see why *he* should be sorry.'

Billy looked at the ring and nodded. 'King has taken Bess. I won't allow harm to come to her. It was her who chipped away at this ring every time it was off Houdini's finger. Trying to disrupt the circuits ...'

'She was helping you?' Graham said.

Billy smiled sadly. 'We helped each other.'

The Doctor had started pacing the stage. 'Well, if Wiseman King has any more of your technology, Billy, my little gadget here ought to ... Yes! There's a trace. Northwest Side ...'

'King owns property in Old Edgebrook District,' Billy said.

'So what are we waiting for?' said Yaz. 'Let's find Ryan and get going!'

Graham nodded. 'Where is he, anyway? He left with Dorothy ...'

We were all in the same car – me, Ryan, Houdini and Mrs H – all with the windows blacked out, cutting across town. I never felt so scared. The car slowed, went through a big set of iron gates and along a winding path into the middle of a wood. Waiting for us there was a fine fancy mansion.

Mrs H looked at her husband. 'You don't have the ring.'

'No,' Houdini murmured. 'When I recognised Dawson, I took it off and switched it for my signet ring, left it for the Doctor to find. If the ring is safe then, when we see King, we'll have something to bargain with.'

'Bargain with that degenerate?' Mrs H shuddered. 'You can't. He's only brought the three of us to use as leverage against you.'

I gulped. 'You mean he'll hurt us?'

'Naw,' Ryan said, with a hard look at Mrs H. He had a bloody cut on his temple but he hadn't complained about it once. 'They thought we were hiding that travel pod thing they loaded onto their truck. Bet you they brought us along cos they think we know how it works.'

'Maybe,' I conceded. 'But I don't see how it came to be in your dressing room, Mrs H.'

'My wife is unnaturally close to the creature,' Houdini said coldly. 'With all the shapes and faces it can assume, she makes it a mirror to her past.'

'You've sought to dominate it with your will as you have everyone else in the world,' Bess said quietly. 'I have simply shown the poor thing understanding … and in return it has shown me what I wished so much to see.'

Her and Houdini when they were young, I realised numbly. When the two of them were starting out. The excitement of the climb, before you reach the top and realise the only way on from there is the slide back down.

I didn't have long to wrap my head around it all. The car lurched to a stop and we were all pulled out by Dawson and his two thugs and steered through a set of fancy French windows into a big sitting room. There were white floorboards and redbrick walls hung with stuffed animal heads and creepy paintings of hellfire landscapes. An old man in a white suit and fedora sat in a high-backed chair; Dawson stood at his right hand while the two hoods hovered on his left, their guns drawn and pointed at us.

The old man started to speak in this low, rasping drawl. 'Hello, Harry. You know you're meant to kneel before royalty, right?'

Houdini inclined his head. 'Wiseman King.'

'Sorry to drag you and your company over here without notice, but I read my horoscope yesterday and it didn't look good. This face-changing freak I used to run my errands is running loose. Now, I was a careful owner.' He leaned forward, narrowed his eyes at Houdini. 'Guess the mug I sold it to wasn't so clever.'

'The ring grows weak, it can't control the creature all the time,' Houdini said. 'That must be why its killing spree began.'

'I can fix the ring. I got a power source right here ready to juice it up.' King took off his hat and mopped his brow with a silk handkerchief. 'You know, I can't believe that all you made that beast do was take part in your lousy act! You're no better than Gladstone – sold him the eye in the sky and he spies with it for his mindreading act.' He leaned forward. 'I had that freak impersonating senators, judges … making laws and breaking 'em.

Getting me dirt on the great and good of this city. I was so, so sad to give the thing away.'

Ryan stepped forward. 'Yeah, well, maybe that's why it's saving you for last?'

'That's not gonna be a problem.' King smiled. 'Houdini, I know you didn't carry that bulletproof cabinet out of Gladstone's lock-up back to the theatre and all the way up to your wife's dressing room. It moves, right – like a car?' He looked between Ryan and me. 'Damn thing would never work when I tried it, but somehow you guys got it to move …'

'We can't drive it, we only found it,' Ryan said.

'We just found the thing in Mrs H's room,' I added, but even I thought I sounded like a liar.

'Look, doll. You're all here because I'm taking back what's mine. The cabinet, the shape-changer …' King beamed at Houdini. 'Hell, your boss is going to write me a real big cheque just to take that monster off his hands! And if you don't cooperate, I start breaking bones.' He nodded to Mrs H. 'Starting with good queen Bess.'

I felt frozen with fear. Mrs H just stuck her chin out at him, cool as you like.

'There's a problem, King,' Houdini said calmly. 'I'm afraid your goons here forgot to bring the ring along with them.'

'What?' King glared at the men either side of him. 'Where the hell is it?'

Dawson, the manservant with the huge grin, wasn't smiling now. 'He had it, sir.' He stepped forward, started patting down Houdini. 'I saw it on him …'

'Seriously? He's Houdini, you blockhead, you weren't expecting sleight of hand?' King was slowly turning puce inside his white suit. 'He won't have it on him. Get on back to the Uptown and you tear the place apart until you come back with—'

'This what you're after?' The patio door swung open and the Doctor strode in, the ring raised in her left hand. 'I found it in the trap space. Clumsy, Harry, dropping it like that!'

'Fix her,' King snarled and his men started forward.

'I wouldn't!' The Doctor produced the pewter wand and tapped the glowing crystal tip against the ring. 'I can scramble this thing in a heartbeat and it'll be no good for anything. So, Mr King, why not go and fetch that power source you mentioned, eh?' She tapped the ring again and it crackled. 'Sorry, long night and I'm not feeling very patient. Could you?'

King had turned waxwork still. Finally he looked at Dawson. 'C'mon,' he said. 'The rest of you – kill Houdini and his wife first if she tries anything.' He rose stiffly and left the room with his aide.

'It's good to see you, Doctor,' I began. 'Where are Yaz and—?'

'Nice to see you too, Dodo!' she cut me off. 'You too, Bessie. Don't worry, things will be fine. Won't they, Ryan?'

Ryan gave her a hopeful smile. 'Fingers crossed, right?'

'Right. Cos no one else is getting hurt today. I've decided.' She tapped the ring with the metal rod once again. 'And your boss, Mr King, I'm sure he's going to see reason.'

The door swung open. Wiseman King came shuffling back inside. He was holding a small metal case in his right hand. Dawson the manservant followed – and he was holding Graham and Yaz at gunpoint! No wonder the Doctor had hushed me up, her friends must have sneaked in from the other direction while she barged in the back.

'Oh, dear,' Bess whispered.

'Oh, my *days*!' Ryan groaned.

'Sorry, Doc, Mrs H, Dorothy.' Graham looked pained. 'We tried to rush 'em, but …'

'Smiling boy here was too fast,' Yaz muttered.

'Nice try, Doctor.' King smiled. 'Now how about you put down your little toy and let us men deal with things – before that freak turns up here, sharpening its claws. Give me the ring or these two trespassers die now.'

'All right.' The Doctor had stopped smiling. 'All right, don't hurt them. I'm throwing the ring across to you now.'

King caught it neatly in one hand. He gave a sigh of satisfaction and placed the metal box down on the table.

Then the old man's body blurred and changed into a huge grey golem of a monster who crushed the ring in one enormous fist.

I screamed, disbelieving, and grabbed Mrs H, dragged her to the floor with me as King's men aimed their guns at the thing, ready to fire.

'Don't think so!' Yaz snatched the gun away from Dawson just as Graham pounced on his friend and wrenched his revolver from his grip. As for the third guy, Ryan shoved him forward and Houdini karate chopped him on the back of the neck. The hood fell to the floor beside me, and groaned. I pulled off my shoe and hit him on the back of the head. He shut up then.

'Nice work, everyone!' The Doctor was back to beaming again.

'Doctor, what's happening!' I shouted. That horrible grey monster was still here and it took a step towards me. I moaned with fear. I actually raised my shoe as if a two-inch heel could do a damn thing. But then my vision blurred again – and it was Billy looking down at me. Billy with those amazing eyes, full of worry, full of passion. Reaching out his arms …

For Mrs H beside me.

Gently he pulled her up. 'You're all right?' he said. 'I was so frightened King would hurt you …'

'It's you,' I said, my voice catching. 'The creature is you.'

'He's a person, Dorothy,' the Doctor said softly. 'Like the rest of us.'

Mrs H shook her head. 'Except for King.'

'Where *is* King?' Houdini gazed coldly at Billy, as his wife awkwardly pulled away from the boy's grip. 'You gave as precise an impersonation of him as you do of me … but you haven't killed him?'

'King'll live,' said Graham. 'Me and Yaz jumped out and let Dawson here chase after us while Billy put the old sod to sleep in his strong room and came out in his place.'

'Now the ring's been destroyed there's no way to control him,' Houdini said. 'He's a killer.'

'I am free,' said Billy.

'And he's leaving,' said the Doctor. 'You understand that, Billy, don't you. Your revenge ends here, no more murders. It's time to go.'

'Why didn't you go before,' I asked, 'if you could?'

'Because I didn't have this.' Billy pressed his hand against the metal of the box. 'This is what I was looking for.'

The box glowed, and suddenly visions filled the drawing room: an alien moon in space struck with strange constellations; grey, spindly figures dancing and waving on an azure beach. Unearthly cries and calls like whale song. Lights wheeling in an alien sky. 'It was all the slavers let us take: memories of home.' He smiled in wonder at the crazy pattern of images. 'Now it's all I have left of my old life. Those I knew and loved will be scattered far away and everywhere by now.'

I remembered Billy asking me in the shop backstage: *'You ever get homesick, Dorothy? The places where you grew, the people you knew – that helped make you what you are . . .?'*

'Now you can go find them, Billy,' the Doctor said. 'Space is a big place, but anything lost can be found.'

'Yes, Doctor.' Billy smiled at Mrs H. 'I believe it can.'

Houdini cleared his throat. 'I know I also must make amends. You will allow me, perhaps, to help you take your cabinet from King's men's truck and ready it for departure?'

Billy stared. 'So, the great Houdini is to assist the stagehand?'

Houdini glanced at his wife. 'It is in both our interests, I think.'

'Very well. I accept your offer.'

'All right, then.' Houdini smiled tightly. 'There is no time like the present, hmm?'

From the look on her face, Mrs H would have preferred pretty much any other time at all.

The Doctor busied herself going through King's strong room. She helped herself to any items she didn't think belonged here, and loaded up Ryan and Yaz with them. Graham managed to manoeuvre King's yellow 1914 Benz 8/20 Tourer out of the garage and onto the drive, and the Doctor got her friends inside, grinning like a maniac.

'I've got form with motors like this,' she said. 'Named one after Mrs H, you know ...'

Bess waited with her husband and Dorothy on King's lawn; all was quiet besides the hoot and call of night creatures in the surrounding woods. Billy stood inside his travel pod, ready to depart: his legs were lost in the curved white metal about him, the crystal casing clamped over his head, shoulders and chest.

'Old Billy's not wasting much time is he?' said Ryan.

'He's been wasting it for decades,' Graham murmured. 'I know he killed those people, but ... well, you do sort of feel for him.'

'He'll face no justice for what he did,' Yaz brooded. 'Nor will Houdini, for that matter.'

'Poor Harry doesn't last out the year,' the Doctor said sadly. 'Dies on Halloween night, 1926. Peritonitis.'

They looked across to the proud, stocky man standing on the lawn beside Bess, who had tears streaming down her face. Dorothy placed her arms around her, and they wept together.

'I suppose,' said Ryan, 'sometimes … all you can do is try to move on.'

The travel pod smoked and hissed and glowed a deep and brilliant red, before it vanished like a hole in the night and burned away.

The Doctor stuck the car in gear and waved to Dorothy and the Houdinis. 'You squeezing in with us?'

'We will follow on,' Houdini called. 'Farewell, Doctor.' He inclined his head. 'And to Ryan, Yasmin and Graham, adieu.'

'The old boy doesn't think I'm beautiful any more.' Graham gave a pantomime sniff. 'It's time to go, all right!'

And go they did. I waved to them, these four strangers who'd tipped my world upside down, and felt suddenly homesick. Not so much for Ocean Grove, New Jersey – more for the simplicity of the life I'd had up till then as plain old Dorothy Smith, the seventeen-year-old showgirl off to see the world. Even in my shock, the way my mind was shying from the things I'd seen, I knew I'd never be the same.

We were still standing there on the lawn, trespassing on Wiseman King's property. He and his thugs were tied up inside (Mrs H always was good with knots) but I only began to feel safe again when we'd driven King's truck back across the city and parked up outside the Uptown. Houdini had wanted to be sure the Doctor's box had gone, and it had. The alley was empty.

'Well, then,' Houdini said. 'It is over. Out you get, Dorothy, my dear.'

I still had the keys that Ryan had used to access all areas, and so I stepped out into the moonlight and the bite of traffic over on North Broadway. I glanced back at the truck and I saw, plain in the silver light, that Houdini was fully twenty years younger beside Mrs H, and the happiness in her face made her look nearly as young herself.

And that's when I worked it out: Billy hadn't gone anywhere. Harry Houdini had performed his last and greatest escape trick. He'd felt trapped by the life he'd carved out at the top and imagined that the only way to go was down. But events these last two days had showed him another way: straight up and out.

'In the end,' Billy'd said to me, *'you have to settle someplace.'* Only for him and Mrs H, I knew it wasn't settling at all.

I kept their secret, while it lasted. It scared me to death, but I knew what Mrs H knew – that Billy wasn't evil, only angry, and born to another time with different laws. Besides, what else could I do? I didn't want the show to spoil, and my time on the road to end. And so we journeyed on, our little company; 'Houdini' and Bess never put on Reincarnation again, of course, but they went back to the old Metamorphosis illusion and it went well every time. We took our greatest show to Ohio, Pennsylvania, Massachusetts, Michigan, to Canada …

But Houdini – Billy, I mean – he died seven months later, in Detroit. Ruptured appendix. Doctors did their best but couldn't fix him.

Mrs H said to me after that Billy was killed in the end by human weakness, and wasn't that just the biggest irony? I never saw her again, but I went on travelling and had my own adventures. I told you, it's the travel that's the greatest.

As for the real Houdini, well, far as I know he never came back. I wonder where he went, flying through creation at the speed of thought? I try to imagine one iota of the things he must have seen . . .

But, you know. The thoughts escape me.

The Pythagoras Problem

Trevor Baxendale

'I feel like a right Charlie in this.'

'Graham, you look *great*,' Yaz assured him, and then turned away so that only Ryan could see her face. She was biting her lip to stop herself laughing.

'It's cool, mate,' Ryan said, a little too innocently. 'Believe me.'

'Why can't we wear our normal gear?' Graham asked.

'Honestly,' said the Doctor, distracted at the control console, 'you'll thank me for it when we arrive.' She was making a series of tiny, last-minute adjustments as she brought the TARDIS into land.

'It's all right for you young'uns,' Graham said to Yaz and Ryan, who were now both trying harder than ever to keep straight faces. 'You'll fit right in. But what am I supposed to do with these?' He pointed at his feet; bare and white in a pair of old leather sandals. He wiggled his toes. 'I'm not even allowed to wear socks!'

Yaz looked at Graham's knobbly knees poking out beneath his toga and giggled again. Yaz and Ryan looked resplendent – as if they were on their way to the ultimate toga party. Next to them, Graham felt like an extra from *Carry On Cleo*.

'Charming,' Graham muttered. 'What about you, Doc? How come you get to keep your usual clobber?'

'I fit in wherever I go,' the Doctor replied with the blithe confidence of the completely self-unaware. 'And *when*ever, for that matter. Talking of which: we've arrived. Come on!'

The giant crystal at the centre of the console had ceased its gentle rise and fall, indicating that the TARDIS had materialised. The Doctor was already halfway to the police box doors.

'Don't forget these, Doctor!' Ryan called, scooping up a pair of sunglasses from the edge of the console.

But the Doctor's cry of 'Hurry up, you lot!' was already drifting in from outside the TARDIS. 'Cor! It's *lovely* here ...'

The sun shone hot and bright from the bluest sky Graham had seen in quite a while. He raised an arm to shield his eyes and reluctantly agreed that, yes, in this kind of heat his toga was actually quite comfortable. Ryan and Yaz were already scrambling down the dusty hillside after the Doctor. 'Oi, wait for me!' Being careful to shut the TARDIS door – someone had to be the responsible one, after all – Graham hurried after them.

'Rome's that way,' announced the Doctor when Ryan asked her exactly where they were. Her arms swung around like a windmill to indicate various directions. 'Sicily that way. Vesuvius over there, somewhere – can't see it from here.'

'Vesuvius?' Graham queried.

'Yeah, not due to erupt for a good few centuries though. Been there, done that. Twice. Oh, look!' The Doctor stopped mid-stride and pointed directly ahead. 'The sea! You can see Greece from here on a clear day.'

They all stopped and admired the glittering blue ocean. It was difficult to imagine a clearer day, but the horizon was lost in a shimmering heat haze. Graham stared at the horizon and blinked, certain his vision was going wobbly.

'Here, Doc,' he said, 'I dunno if it's the heat or what but I don't feel so good.'

Yaz and Ryan turned to look at Graham as he bent forward, hands resting on his knees.

'What's up?' Ryan asked.

'Bit woozy, that's all.' Graham held a hand out to show he didn't need any help. 'I'll be fine in a minute. I just need a moment.'

'You're getting old, that's your problem,' Ryan joked.

'Hey,' the Doctor said. 'No cracks about advancing years, if you don't mind. Besides, it's not the heat that's affecting Graham. I felt something too – like a sudden shift in the localised time-space continuum. Didn't you feel it?'

Yaz and Ryan shook their heads. 'Not really.'

The Doctor looked puzzled. 'What? Nothing? No sudden nausea? Not even butterflies?'

A bright yellow butterfly floated along the ground by Ryan and then fluttered innocently away into the distance. Yaz shrugged. 'I just thought it was that Draconian buffet we had last night.'

'Oh man.' Ryan pulled a face. 'Them jellyrat scallops. I was up half the night.'

'There's something funny going on here,' the Doctor said, scanning the horizon carefully. Her voice was suddenly serious, as cool as a passing cloud. 'Give Graham a hand and keep your wits about you.'

'But we're definitely in Italy?' Yaz said a little later, when Graham was feeling better and they could continue their stroll down the hillside. The sun was heading for the edge of the world and the shadows were getting longer, but it was still very warm.

'Of course!' The Doctor sounded as if the matter could never have been in doubt. She strode on with a similar confidence, her boots kicking up clouds of dust. '500 BC, give or take. Right on target.'

'And we're really going to meet Pythagoras?' Bumping into the great and the good (and sometimes the awful and the bad) from Earth's history was something of an occupational hazard when travelling in the TARDIS, but Yaz couldn't imagine she would ever tire of it.

'That's the plan,' replied the Doctor, setting off down the hill towards the coast. 'Crotone is this way. That's where he's living around now, with his Pythagorean commune, teaching theoretical maths and stuff.'

'He sounds like a barrel of laughs,' Graham said.

'Never did like maths,' Ryan said.

'The square of the hypotenuse is equal to the sum of the squares of the other two sides,' Yaz recited. 'That's his special theorem – I remember it from school. Not sure I've ever *needed* to remember it, though. Until now.'

'Oh, there's loads more to Pythagoras than maths,' the Doctor said. 'He's a philosopher, traveller, astronomer, mystic, metempsychologist ...'

'Metem-what?' Graham asked.

'He believes in reincarnation, Graham – metempsychosis.' The Doctor paused to look at them with a twinkle in her eye. 'And he's not far off the mark.'

'Heads up,' said Ryan, pointing further down the hillside. 'Welcome party.'

A group of men were struggling up the slope carrying a dead weight. They grunted and cursed with the effort, and then dropped whatever they were carrying on the ground in a cloud of dust.

'There you go!' one of the men growled. 'Have a night in the dirt and see you in the morning!' He aimed a kick at the shape on the ground and then led his fellows off back down the hill towards the village.

The Doctor, Ryan and Yaz hurried down to where the shape lay groaning. By the time Graham caught up – running in sandals wasn't easy – they were helping a very old man into a sitting position. His white hair was tangled, his beard was matted with food and he stank of booze.

'He's a bit worse for wear, ain't he?' Graham chuckled.

'Drunk as a newt,' Yaz confirmed. She'd seen enough of them on a Friday night in Sheffield city centre.

'Wonder who he is?' said Ryan. 'Looks like the town wino.'

'Oi – this is my old mate,' the Doctor protested, concerned. 'Pythagoras!'

The Doctor and Yaz helped the old man to his feet, where he swayed for a moment and then fixed Graham with an accusatory, if somewhat bleary, stare. 'Ghosts!' he said, loudly and distinctly. 'The souls of the dead!'

'You sure this is Pythagoras?' asked Ryan. 'I mean, great thinker ...?'

'They're lost! And in torment!' the old man insisted dourly, before ruining the moment with a loud belch. 'Souls of the dead, y'hear!'

'It's the booze talking,' said Yaz. 'Come on, let's get him home. Give us a hand, Ryan. He's heavier than he looks.'

Ryan slipped one of the man's arms around his neck and helped take the weight. 'Where to, bro?' he asked Pythagoras.

'It's all right, I know the way,' declared the Doctor, and headed off down the hill towards the village.

Back, Graham noted, in the direction the villagers had come from when they dumped the old geezer in the dirt like a sack of rubbish. The setting sun picked out the low terracotta roofs of Crotone in a deep red glow, as if the whole town was ablaze.

'Decent crib,' Ryan said a little later as they looked around the villa. It wasn't huge, but it was light and airy and had an excellent view of the Ionian Sea from the terrace. It was a hot Mediterranean evening and Ryan was thankful for his toga and sandals. Somewhere there was a dog barking, but otherwise everything was quiet and peaceful. Ryan wasn't fooled for a minute, though;

the Doctor's unerring nose for trouble would inevitably put paid to that.

The Doctor sat on a stone bench with Pythagoras, who was nursing a very sore head.

'Here,' said the Doctor. 'Try these. They're yours anyway. I was returning them.' She handed him the sunglasses. 'I'm terrible for borrowing stuff, me.'

The sunglasses were a fancy leopard-pattern design, and Pythagoras eyed them suspiciously. 'Are you sure?'

'Just put them on, your eyes look awful.' The Doctor helped him put the sunglasses on.

'Oh! That's quite remarkable,' the old man said, perking up a little as he peered around the room through the Polaroid lenses. 'My poor head feels better already.'

'Smashing. Now, what have you been drinking for? What's all this about ghosts?'

'Spirits! The tormented souls—'

'—of the dead, yes, so you said. I didn't believe it then, and I don't believe it now, quite frankly.'

'Oh but it is true, Doctor,' Pythagoras insisted. 'I swear to you. I have felt the anguish of these spirits. Witnessed their suffering! It is as though something has gripped my own soul and squeezed it hard in a fist of pure ice.'

'The only spirits you've seen have been in a bottle, mate,' said Graham, although his smile was forced. The old man's description, his *soul being squeezed in a fist of ice,* was very similar to what Graham had felt on the hillside earlier that afternoon.

Pythagoras glared at him, although the effect was lost a bit through the sunglasses. 'I know what I'm talking about.'

'Maybe he does,' Yaz shrugged. 'I mean, we've seen a fair few weird things, haven't we? Who's to say ghosts aren't real?'

'Me,' said the Doctor emphatically. 'At least not the kind of ghosts he means.'

'But these souls – they are in torment!' Pythagoras insisted.

'Something is,' the Doctor agreed. 'And I'd very much like to know what.'

Outside, the dog was still barking ten to the dozen. Something had spooked it all right. Ryan looked back out into the gathering darkness. He could see lights flickering in the distance, presumably other houses or villas. But beyond that the night was gathering, the stars were out, and the moon was full. Did dogs bark at the moon?

'Can you hear him?' Pythagoras asked. 'That dog?'

They all nodded. 'Surprised the neighbours don't complain with that racket going on all night,' Graham added.

'They do. But the other day I stopped that very dog from being beaten in the street, because I recognised someone I once knew in its voice.'

The Doctor's eyes opened wider than ever. 'Really?'

'Oh yes. My dear, departed friend, Tylos. In the hound's every yelp and snap, I could hear Tylos's own words – although I could not understand what he said.'

'Get away!' Ryan said. He wasn't buying that for a minute.

'I'm serious,' Pythagoras snapped. 'I know I am not mistaken. I can still hear him now. He's in the courtyard. I had to chain him up.'

They all listened to the frantic barking of the dog.

'You see, all souls are immortal. When we die, the soul is transferred to another body – a new body. It's an endless cycle of renewal and rebirth.'

'Metempsychosis,' Yaz remembered. 'Was that what you said, Doctor?'

Pythagoras laughed at this, and then winced, holding his head. 'The Doctor is living proof of my theory, as no doubt you've learned.'

'There's a little bit more to bodily regeneration than you think, Pythagoras,' said the Doctor. 'Not everyone can do it – and I'm pretty sure that dog *isn't* the reincarnation of one of your mates.' Her eyes widened again as a thought struck her. 'Ooh! Can I have a look at him? The dog, I mean?'

It was a brindle-furred mongrel of the kind seen all over the world for centuries. Graham identified it immediately: 'Heinz 57.'

'You what?' Ryan frowned.

'Fifty-seven different varieties,' Graham explained. 'Honestly, don't you kids know anything any more?'

'I know how to wear a toga.'

'Oi,' Graham tried to rearrange his robes into a more dignified look.

The dog was exhausted from all the barking. Its tongue lolled between its jaws and its eyes were wild. Firelight from the wall torches illuminating the courtyard glimmered on its foam-flecked jaws.

'Here,' Graham said cautiously, 'it's not got rabies or something, has it?'

The Doctor scanned the dog with her sonic screwdriver. 'No sign of any virus or infection. In fact it's pretty healthy – apart from the fleas.'

The dog gave an anguished howl.

'My poor old friend,' Pythagoras said sadly. 'Tylos's very soul is trapped inside a mad dog.'

'Don't be daft,' the Doctor said, maintaining eye contact with the animal. 'There's some … energy in this doggy all right. But it isn't human – not even remotely.'

'It's alien?' asked Yaz, intrigued.

'Perhaps.' The Doctor checked the sonic again. 'This isn't telling me much.'

'So what's up with him?' Graham wondered.

The mongrel growled and bared its yellow teeth again.

'Careful,' said Ryan as the Doctor bent closer. 'It could be faking – if it's an alien, I mean. Waiting for you to get closer. I saw this film once where—'

Suddenly everyone in the room seemed to stop, draw a single breath and then look at one another. They had all experienced it – a sudden feeling of sickness, as if everything in the world had just changed, but invisibly. Graham put a hand over his mouth. 'There it is again,' he groaned. 'Here, Doc, I think I'm coming down with somethin'.'

The Doctor was wide-eyed, holding her hands out as if trying to regain her balance. 'No, it was just another flux in the local continuum. I felt it too. What about you two?'

Ryan and Yaz both nodded.

'Horrible,' Yaz said. 'I feel dizzy.'

'I've had some bad nights out,' Ryan commented, 'but I've never felt like that.'

'There's something very not right here,' the Doctor said.

'Don't touch that animal!' shrieked a young woman as she came hurtling into the yard. She flew straight between the Doctor and the dog, pushing her arms out to try and separate them. Her green eyes burned with anger.

Pythagoras turned to the Doctor. 'I'm so sorry about this, Doctor. Allow me to introduce my daughter – Myia.'

'Pleased to meet you, Myia,' said the Doctor.

'Do not touch this … thing,' said Myia, pointing at the dog. It snarled and then, quite suddenly, flattened its ears and tried to press itself down into the dirt. 'It is dangerous!'

In the light of the flickering torches, the dog's eyes had taken on a strange, golden hue – almost as if they were glowing from within. Graham knew that light could sometimes play tricks with the eyes of animals, making them shine at night, but this was something quite different – not least because, as the dog looked up at Myia, the light seemed to be reflected in her eyes as well.

Then the dog's eyes went dark and it let out a tired whimper.

The Doctor frowned. 'It's just frightened,' she said, steadily and clearly. 'I don't think it's going to attack anyone.'

The woman glared at her, her eyes still bright in the night. 'Who are you? What do you want here?'

'This is my good friend, the Doctor,' explained Pythagoras. 'You've met her before. But she looked somewhat different then, and you were very young, and probably don't remember. The Doctor and her friends are always honoured guests in my house, Myia, and I would like you to remember that.'

'We just want to help,' Yaz told her kindly.

'If you want to help, you should leave.' Myia turned on Pythagoras. 'You and your obsessions. You have led your followers into dark sorcery – and your family too!'

'Steady on, love,' suggested Graham kindly. 'Cup of tea and a little sit down. Do you the world of good.'

'Dark sorcery?' repeated the Doctor.

'No, Doc, *cup of tea,*' said Graham.

Miya looked at the Doctor. 'He was initiated into the Ancient Rites by the Egyptian wizard Thoth,' she declared. 'He'll infect us all with his foreign beliefs!'

'That's all complete nonsense,' Pythagoras protested.

'Did you or did you not meet with the dark priests of Egypt?'

'I studied under Oenuphis in Egypt – geometry, metempsychosis and philosophy. Not black magic.'

'I have heard you speak with the tongue of a demon! You commune with the beasts of the night!'

Pythagoras sighed. 'I studied with the Persian magi in Babylon and learned many new languages. None of them have afforded me communication with evil spirits – until now, and this poor wretched animal. Whatever has possessed you, Myia? This isn't like you at all.'

'Don't try to blame all this on me,' his daughter snarled, and then, with an exasperated cry, she pushed past him and ran from the courtyard. 'Will no one understand?'

Pythagoras was clearly distressed. The Doctor shot Yaz a look and she nodded her understanding. 'I'll go after her, check she's all right.'

'Something's definitely not right here, Pythagoras,' the Doctor said as Yaz left.

The old man sat down heavily on a bench. 'I know. And it's getting worse.'

Yaz found Myia in her room on the other side of the villa, sitting on a low stone bench with her arms wrapped tight around her knees. When Myia sensed Yaz in the room, she sat up straight and cleared her throat.

'Hey,' said Yaz gently.

Myia sniffed angrily. 'What do you want?'

'Only to help, if I can.' Yaz leaned against the doorway. 'Like, what was all that about? You've had more than a bad day, yeah? Anyone can see that.'

'It's nothing,' Myia said, tight-lipped. She picked up a handful of pebbles from a nearby flowerpot and started to grind them in her fist like some sort of stress reliever.

'Oh come on,' Yaz pressed a little harder. She'd had training in how to talk to witnesses and suspects. 'I know what it's like when your dad's driving you crazy with the latest stupid scheme, believe me. What's up?'

'He's mad. All that nonsense about reincarnation, about hearing his friend speaking through the hound, saving it from a beating . . .' Myia stared into the distance as she spoke. 'My father drove away the men who had been beating the dog, cursing them for devils and fools.

He was very brave. He saved its life, I don't doubt that. But he only cared for the soul of the man he thought was trapped inside, and not for the animal itself. And he never stopped to wonder why those men were beating it.'

'Do you know?'

She nodded. 'Of course. They knew it was possessed by a demon. They were trying to kill it. When they found out he'd saved it they dragged him out of town and left him to rot.'

The Doctor was kneeling down close to the dog, gently rubbing at the fur behind its ear. 'What's up with you, eh?' she asked softly. The animal was completely docile now, without a trace of its previous bad temper. In the flickering golden light of the yard torches, it looked positively tame. 'What's the matter? You can tell me, I'm the Doctor.'

The Doctor rested her forehead against that of the dog and closed her eyes.

'Don't tell me you can talk to the animals,' said Graham in disbelief.

'Wrong Doctor,' Ryan told him.

'Hush, you two,' said the Doctor. She sounded very worried, and both Ryan and Graham were instantly on alert.

'This could be it,' Ryan hissed anxiously. 'Like in the film, man. When it turns out the alien's a shape-changer and it just *looks* like a dog ...'

The Doctor waved him to silence. She looked stricken; her eyes were always expressive, but whereas they were normally full of gleeful wonder at any new experience, they were now dark with concern.

The dog had closed its eyes and rested its head on the floor next to the Doctor. She continued to stroke the fur on its neck with a gentle hand.

'What's going on?' Pythagoras asked quietly, but everyone in the room knew only too well and suddenly the air felt heavy.

The Doctor gave a sad shake of her head. 'I'm so sorry, Pythagoras.' She gave the dog a gentle, final pat.

Pythagoras gave a small gasp. 'Is he—'

She nodded. 'He's gone. He's at peace now.'

Ryan and Graham glanced at each other. This was too awful. Graham poured a goblet of wine for Pythagoras. 'Wasn't there anything you could do, Doc?'

'No,' the Doctor replied simply, still sitting on her haunches by the body of the dog.

'Poor Tylos,' said Pythagoras, gratefully gulping the wine. 'The life that had been inside that stray ... the soul ... I knew him. I *knew* him.'

'It may have *sounded* like someone you knew,' said the Doctor thoughtfully, 'but it wasn't.'

Ryan frowned. 'You mean it was something *pretending* to be someone he knew?'

The Doctor took out her sonic screwdriver once more and used it to scan the body. She checked the results and glanced back at the animal in puzzlement. 'That's odd.'

'Isn't everything these days?' wondered Graham, but then he was frowning too – because the dog was starting to change. Its overall shape didn't alter, but there was something about the fur that looked distinctly odd. The pelt seemed to wither away, and the skin beneath it crystallise, and then crack and cave in on itself, as if the underlying flesh and bone had suddenly lost all solidity. The dog simply crumbled away in front of them, until all that remained was a mound of grit.

'By all the gods!' exclaimed Pythagoras, aghast.

'What ... just happened?' asked Ryan, shocked.

'I'm not sure,' said the Doctor, checking the sonic again. 'It's almost like the binding forces within the entire molecular structure just sort of ... stopped. Which is impossible. I mean possible, obviously, because it's just happened right in front of us. But I've never seen or heard of anything like that before.'

'What could cause it?' asked Graham.

'Nothing in this universe.'

A sudden chill seemed to pass through the courtyard, although there was no breeze. The night air was still and dark.

'You said your dad was into ... what, black magic and stuff?' Yaz said. 'The Egyptian priest ...?'

'Thoth,' said Myia bitterly. She played around with the pebbles from a plant pot a little more. 'I don't know what my father actually did in Egypt. No one does. He lived there for ten years, and the Pharaoh himself taught him how to speak Egyptian.'

'He must be very clever.'

'Oh, he is. Everyone knows the great Pythagoras! He studied with the priests in Thebes and was the only foreigner ever to be granted the privilege of taking part in their worship. He travelled to India where he was trained by the Hindu sages. He learned from the Iberians and the Celts. I truly believe that no one in all the world knows more than my father.'

'Yeah, but black magic?'

Myia shrugged. 'He must have learned something of the darker arts. His head is full of all kinds of wild ideas. Now students come from all over the world to join him here and study under him. He has very strict rules, though. Not everyone can bear them. Some cannot understand why he allows women to study mathematics and philosophy with him.'

'Well, good on him,' said Yaz with feeling.

'My mother was his first female student. My own husband was a close associate.'

Yaz raised an eyebrow. 'Keeping it in the family, eh?'

'We are a community.' Myia started to move the pebbles around on the bench, absentmindedly pushing one here or there in a random geometric pattern.

'Well, community's important. And so is family. And I know they can drive you mad at times. But to say that your dad's channelling demons from Egypt because he thinks his mate's come back as a dog ...' Yaz paused. 'It was funny, how it seemed to calm down when you were there.'

'It did, didn't it?' Myia went on staring at the pebbles. 'Perhaps I have an affinity with those who suffer.'

Pythagoras had found a sheet to put over the crystalline remains of the dog. Then he called for his son-in-law,

Milo, to take it away, briefly describing exactly what had happened.

Milo was what Ryan would call 'a unit'. His arms were corded with muscle, his chest was massive and his neck thick. In any other circumstances Ryan might have marked him down as trouble, but there was a keen intelligence at work behind the big man's eyes.

'It's been quite the day for strange goings-on,' Milo said as he gently gathered the remains together.

'Really?' said the Doctor. 'Such as? Don't be shy, I love strange goings-on, me. Stranger the better, in fact, because this business is really scoring high on my strange-o-meter.'

Milo shrugged his huge shoulders. 'Weird stuff. First this poor thing – speaking in voices, so I'm told, and now collapsing into so much dust. Then there's the blue box that appeared up on the hillside …'

'Oh, you don't need to worry about that, cockle,' said Graham quickly.

'No,' the Doctor agreed. 'But there is something else, isn't there? It's got your wife wound up, for sure.'

Milo pulled a face, undecided. 'Well, there is the business with the tetractys appearing in unexpected places …'

'The what?' said Ryan.

'My geometrical representation of the fourth triangular number,' Pythagoras enthused. 'Ten equal points arranged in four rows of four, three, two and one.'

'Whoa,' Ryan said, holding up his hands in surrender. 'I smell maths.'

'The tetractys is a mystical symbol for all followers of Pythagoras.' Milo took up a slate and a piece of chalk and, with the help of the torchlight, started to make a series of large dots to represent the ten points of the diagram. 'Four, then three, then two, then one; like this.'

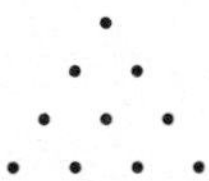

'We believe it represents the four seasons, as well as planetary motion and music. It works the same way from whichever angle you look at it – the perfect equilateral, starting with the profound and pure number one until it reaches the holy four, and together they form the mother number – ten.'

'The all-comprising, all-binding and never-tiring holy ten,' Pythagoras added solemnly, as if intoning a prayer.

Ryan squinted at the diagram from various sides. 'Oh yeah. Cool.'

'Looks like one of them puzzles,' Graham said, 'when you have to take away three matchsticks and make it into a square.'

'Match sticks?' Milo echoed.

'There's another aspect of the tetractys that Pythagoras hasn't mentioned yet,' the Doctor said quickly, circling the slate and its ten equally-spaced dots with what could only be described as great caution. 'The first dot represents zero dimensions. The second row – the two dots – represents one dimension, as if there's a line drawn between them. The third row represents two dimensions, and the fourth row three.'

Graham and Ryan were both looking a little lost. 'Sorry Doc,' said Graham, making a whooshing sound and passing a hand right over his head.

'Together these separate and important dimensional forces can be made to interact with the right kind of key,' explained the Doctor – not altogether successfully, if the puzzled looks on her friends' faces were anything to go by. She drew a huge triangular shape in the air with her hands. 'A key to unlock a doorway!'

'A doorway between dimensions?' queried Pythagoras. 'Isn't that a bit fanciful?'

'A moment ago you were telling us this shape is a divine symbol,' said the Doctor sharply.

'I'm not saying I understand any of the maths stuff and that,' said Ryan, 'but I still don't see what it's got to do with that dog.'

The Doctor clicked her fingers and pointed at him. 'Asking all the right questions whether you understand what's going on or not – ten out of ten, Ryan Sinclair!'

'But a doorway to where, exactly?' wondered Graham.

'Ah, always thinking of the practicalities,' beamed the Doctor. 'A doorway, perhaps, to a whole other universe ... and Milo says he's been seeing this pattern all over the place recently. I wonder why?'

At that moment Yaz came into the yard in a state of some frustration. 'I had a chat with Myia and I can tell you she is *fuming*.'

'Excuse me?' said Milo, instantly defensive.

'This is Milo,' Graham explained to Yaz. 'Myia's his missus. There's been a few things going on here.'

'My wife is of the sweetest and most gentle character,' said Milo, still bristling a little.

'Well she might be all milk and honey for you,' Yaz said, 'but at the moment she's more worried about demons trying to – wait, what's that?'

Yaz had stopped dead and was pointing at Milo's slate, still showing the ten dots in triangular formation.

'This is the tetractys,' said Pythagoras proudly.

'It's maths and stuff,' explained Ryan.

'And – in the right circumstances – the nexus points for a dimensional portal,' said the Doctor.

Yaz looked at each of them as if wondering who was telling the truth and who was pulling her leg. She was wise enough to know that they were, in all probability, all telling the truth.

'It's just that I've seen that design somewhere else,' she told them. 'Only a minute ago – Myia was making that exact pattern out of pebbles.'

'What do you want?' Myia demanded when the Doctor swept into her room. She was followed by Yaz, Ryan and Graham, then Pythagoras and Milo.

'Quite the deputation,' Myia said stiffly. She was standing by the window. On the floor in front of her were the pebbles, arranged in the shape of the tetractys.

'Don't touch that!' Myia barked as the Doctor moved towards it.

'Myia, my darling – what has happened to you?' Milo stepped forward, his deep set eyes full of concern. 'What is the matter?'

'I think I know,' said the Doctor. 'That dog ... the way it quietened when you came to it. Whatever was inhabiting its poor little skin – some kind of quantum life form, by my reckoning – has transferred itself to Myia. Is that right, Myia?'

'You're possessed!' Myia spat back.

'Not me,' the Doctor assured her gently. 'You. But I can help.'

Ryan could see that Myia's behaviour was replicating that of the dog – cornered and afraid, expressing itself the one way it could: snapping and barking to keep the strangers at bay. Now Myia, as a human being, was backed up against the dark window, teeth bared like an animal. Her eyes were on fire. 'Keep away from me!' she snarled.

'There's no way out that way,' the Doctor said. 'Only through this ...' She pointed at the tetractys on the floor. 'But it's not working, is it, Myia? Not like it should. That's no portal to another dimension. It's just a pile of stones on the floor.'

Myia hissed angrily, but the Doctor held the woman's fiery gaze. 'I can help you,' she repeated. 'But I need to speak to what's inside you, Myia. It was in the dog, and now it's in you. Maybe it's lost, frightened, I don't know. But it's destroying you and you don't even know. I have to talk to it.'

All the while the Doctor had held the woman's gaze without blinking, taking one slow step forwards at a time. Now she was close enough to reach out and touch her; but instead she simply pulled out the key to the TARDIS from her coat pocket and held it up in front of Myia's eyes.

'Look at this key,' said the Doctor calmly. 'It's the key to another kind of portal. Another dimension, a different universe. Sound familiar? Keep looking at it. See how it shines? Keeping looking at it ...'

The Doctor's voice had dropped to a low, mesmerising intonation. Yaz found herself blinking hard to stay awake. When she glanced at Ryan, she saw his eyes fluttering too and nudged him with an elbow. He woke up with a start just as Graham started to snore. Ryan elbowed him awake.

'I'm OK, I'm OK,' Graham said, blinking hurriedly.

'Everything is calm,' said the Doctor softly, still keeping eye contact with Myia. 'Everything is peaceful. We'll keep it that way until I say otherwise, OK?'

Myia nodded, utterly pacified.

The Doctor put the key away and licked her lips. 'Who am I talking to, by the way?'

I am Zaris of the Argomeld

The voice came from everywhere and nowhere, fading in and out of reality like a badly tuned radio signal. But everyone in the room felt the sudden wave of nausea and a lurch in their stomachs as if they'd stepped off a kerb without realising it. It was a repeat of the same sensations they had felt before, but this time much worse.

'Argomeld?' repeated the Doctor, apparently the only person not to feel queasy. 'That's a new one to me – which is *great*. I love meeting new people. Hello, Zaris. I'm the Doctor.'

I am lost

'I thought so. Where have you come from, Zaris? How do we get you home?'

I am tetractys

'OK, well, communication is obviously a bit limited. And I can't help noticing that Myia – that's the human being you've inhabited – is looking rather poorly. So if you don't mind I'd like to get you out of her, and back to where you belong, as quickly as possible. Does that sound good to you?'

I am tetractys

Graham was feeling very wobbly now and could really do with a sit down. Ryan and Yaz were holding on to each other for support, and Pythagoras and Milo were both looking sickly. Graham was glad he wasn't the only one; he didn't like being a weak link. 'Can it understand you, Doc?'

'I think so,' the Doctor replied. She slowly raised her sonic screwdriver and used it to scan Myia. 'I'm checking right across the dimensional spectrum. I need to know what kind of creature an Argomeld is.'

I am lost

This time the words felt louder, stronger, and they all doubled up in sudden pain. The room seemed to ripple and distort, as if the walls were both receding and closing in at the same time.

'Whoa!' said the Doctor. 'Keep it down, Zaris! You're talking through a time-space continuum and it's bending the local dimensions.'

Tetractys

'Yes, got that: tetractys. It's the way home for you, isn't it? But I need more information. How did you get here in the first place?'

The room warped around them. Graham and Pythagoras sat down heavily on the floor, and Graham put his head in his hands. Yaz and Ryan sank to their knees with their eyes tightly shut as everything began to swim and swirl around them – lines distorting from two dimensions into three and three into four.

I am nothing

I am something

I am …

I am a creeping thing

'Anyone got a bucket cos I'm gonna hurl any minute now,' Graham said.

The Doctor patted him on the shoulder. 'Sit tight, Graham. I think I've got it now.'

I am … crawling

I am … snapping

'All right, Zaris, that's enough,' gasped the Doctor. 'You're going to do permanent damage to local space-time if we carry on much longer.'

I am … human …?

'Not quite, but I can see why you're confused …'

I am tetractys … you are tetractys

'OK, Myia, time to wake up!' the Doctor snapped her fingers a few times and, with a loud gasp, as if she had been holding her breath for all this time, Myia staggered forwards and collapsed into her arms. The room snapped back into its proper shape and dimensions.

Gradually everybody regained their balance and senses. Graham, lips clamped shut and looking very green, gave the Doctor a shaky thumbs up.

*

'It was like an earthquake in the soul.' A few minutes later, Pythagoras was picking over what they'd been through with a detached fascination. 'I have never experienced anything like it. Well, except once, in Persia, when I inhaled—'

'I think we'll skip over that,' interrupted the Doctor. She was pacing the room while the others gathered their wits.

Myia, looking pale, sat with her husband as he urged her to take a sip of wine. 'It will help fortify you for what lies ahead,' Milo explained, but she shook her head silently.

'Probably can't face it,' said Graham, sitting at the window where he could get some fresh air. 'Can't say I blame her, mate. I don't think I'll eat for a week.'

'That'll be the day,' said Ryan.

'Doctor, what's going on?' asked Yaz. 'What was that … thing?'

'Argomeld. I could understand a bit more of what it was trying to say than you could, because I could read the timelines as it affected the real-world continuum. Basically it's an entity derived from quantum mathematics. I think it locks on to life in our universe at a molecular level, a tiny mathematical DNA sequence maybe, insinuating itself into the simplest form of life, a single-celled organism. Then it starts a series of transmigrations, moving from one physical form to another, each more complex and sophisticated than the last … leapfrogging up the food chain … a worm, a rodent, and then maybe a dog – before finally transferring to a human being. The Argomeld will use the human to power its final transference through a tetractic teleport.'

'You mean this thing came to Earth as a microbe or something and then kept jumping from one animal to another? Getting bigger all the time?'

'Pretty much.'

'Good job there's no elephants around here,' said Ryan.

'Size doesn't matter, Ryan. It's the complexity of the brain and the potential for using it. The Argomeld can barely communicate with us now, and it's in a human brain. All it needs is to manufacture a suitable tetractys and then it can transfer back to its home universe or dimension.'

'It said it was a tetractys,' Yaz recalled with a frown.

'It's a mathematical construct – same thing, different arrangement of numbers. Don't ask me to explain block transfer computations to you now because we haven't got a couple of decades to spare.'

'But it said *you* were a tetractys too. Just before you broke the connection.'

'Yeah,' the Doctor frowned. 'I think it could tell I was a more complex space-time event than anything else around here and was trying to identify me.'

'But what's it even doing here in the first place?' asked Graham.

'I don't know. Maybe coming into our universe was an accident. Maybe it's part of its natural life cycle. Maybe Earth just happened to be on the doorstep when the Argomeld came through. There's no way of telling.'

'But surely if it can just leave using the tetra-thingummy it's OK?'

'Yeah,' said Ryan. 'Why doesn't it just hurry up and push off?'

'It will go just as soon as it can,' the Doctor assured them. 'But it's possible that will damage this whole area of space-time.'

'What? Why?'

'You all felt it the disruption when it was just communicating with us,' said the Doctor. 'Imagine what it'll be like when it uses the portal. It could turn the whole planet inside out.'

'So we've got to stop it,' Graham said.

'It can't stay here, Graham.'

'Then we find a way to help it clear off without damaging the space-time whatsit.'

'Yeah,' the Doctor agreed.

There was something about the Doctor's solemn tone that alerted Yaz. 'But it's not as simple as that, is it?'

She shook her head sadly. 'Even if we could find a way to contain the damage to the space-time continuum, you all know what happened to the dog after the Argomeld left it.'

Ryan and Graham looked at each other. They'd told Yaz all about it. Pythagoras and Milo looked equally shocked.

'You mean, Myia will … die?' Milo asked.

'The transference process destabilises the host's atomic structure.'

'But the dog just sort of … collapsed,' Ryan said. 'Into nothing.'

'I know.'

'You can't let this happen to Myia,' Pythagoras croaked.

Milo rose to his feet, fists clenched and muscles quivering. 'I will not let it happen!'

'We may not be able to stop it,' the Doctor said. 'If I'm right, the Argomeld is close to making the jump back to its own universe. Once that happens there will be nothing we can do to help Myia. The process will be complete.'

'This is monstrous!' Pythagoras declared. 'I will not have it! There must be some way – some theorem, some practical solution . . .!'

'Surely the key to this is the tetra-whatsit,' said Graham. 'If she don't have that, the thing inside her can't make the jump home.'

Yaz nodded. 'He's right – so why don't we just stop Myia making the tetractys?'

'Actually,' replied the Doctor, 'I was thinking of helping her.'

They all started talking at once, with Pythagoras and Milo leading the protests, but the Doctor shushed them all as quickly as she could.

'I know it sounds daft,' she said, 'but at least hear me out. Because otherwise Myia doesn't stand a chance, and, to be honest, I don't think the rest of us do either.'

Silence and puzzled looks.

'You all saw what it was like when the Argomeld communicated with us – the block transfer mathematics distorted reality all around us. Remember that it'll be worse when it makes the final tetractys and shifts back to its own plane of existence, leaving this area of the space-time continuum with irreparable damage.'

'But you want to help it do that?' Ryan asked, totally bewildered.

The Doctor nodded eagerly. 'I want to make the transmigration *easier*. If we can reduce the trauma it may not be fatal to Myia and it may prevent the damage to our part of time and space.'

'If? May?' said Milo. 'I do not like these words, Doctor!'

'They're great words, Milo, because they give us *hope*. All we really need is the perfect kind of tetractys. And I've got an idea about that.'

'But Doctor,' argued Pythagoras, 'how can we know what kind of tetractys to make? If the dimensions are so crucial, how can we possibly—'

The Doctor was striding purposefully around the room, hands gesticulating as she tried to describe what she was thinking. 'It's not so much about the measurements, Pythagoras. We could go on refining those until we get down to ten absolute singularities in perfect equilateral tension. I mean that would *work*, of course, but we don't have the tools for that in 500 BC. No, what I have in mind requires a bit more imagination.'

Half an hour later, Myia was standing right in the centre of the outer courtyard of the Pythagoras villa. The Doctor handed her a flaming torch. 'Hold this and stand perfectly still.'

Behind the Doctor stood Pythagoras and Milo, and both of them held torches. Beyond them stood Yaz,

Ryan and Graham, and they had torches too. The flickering light of the flames cast long shadows on the walls of the villa, creating a fervid, threatening atmosphere. No one looked happy to be there, including the three students who stood at the very back of the yard. They also held torches, and the light glistened on their sweating faces. They were Pythagoras's best students and they were being entrusted with the most important task of their lives.

'Right you lot,' the Doctor said to them as she breezed over. 'Aristaeus, you stand here.' She led the first student over to a spot on the far side of the yard. 'Brontinus, you come over here.' The second student shot over to the place she marked and stood there with his torch like a guard on sentry duty, marvelling that the Doctor had remembered his name and mentally promising her his eternal devotion. 'And finally, Pythena, you stand over here. Yes, that's right – there's the spot. Smashing! Brilliant!'

Nine people stood spread across the yard in a broad equilateral triangle. The Doctor took up her position right at the centre; turning on her heel to inspect everyone was in place.

'Are you sure this is gonna work, Doc?' asked Graham plaintively.

'Course!' she replied, crossing the fingers on her free hand. She waved the flaming torch around with the other. 'Giant tetractys made out of people. Perfect!'

'Is it perfect, though?' Pythagoras asked. 'The mathematical relationship must be exact. We can't possibly be totally accurate if—'

'Remember, it's not the exact measurements that matter now,' the Doctor said. 'Just the shape. The positions – and the points of light as the focus. The Argomeld will do the rest. I hope.'

'But how will this help Myia?' Yaz asked.

'Well, I'm hoping that by sharing the transference process among everyone here we can dilute the trauma and Myia can survive.'

'You're hoping?' Ryan echoed uncertainly.

'Sometimes hope is all we have, Ryan.'

'Will it be bad, though?' Yaz asked.

The Doctor looked her straight in the eye. 'I think so, yes. Still up for it?'

Yaz squared her shoulders. 'Yes. I'm ready.'

I am ready

'Ay up, it's starting!' exclaimed the Doctor. 'Everyone – hold your positions and don't move, whatever happens. If anyone breaks the tetractys it's all over. Wait a sec.' She suddenly shot out of position and darted across to Myia at the tip of the triangle. 'Are you ready for this? Cos I am.'

Myia nodded, pale in the light of her torch.

'Brilliant!' the Doctor clapped her on the arm and ran back to her position at the centre as a wind sprang up from nowhere and causes the flames of every torch to flutter and spark. 'Here we go!'

I am tetractys

The voice echoed through the very substance of their being, each one of them channelling the presence of the Argomeld. It was, thought Graham miserably, like being a human tuning fork and picking up on the sound vibrations from a nearby motorway. His teeth didn't feel so much on edge as actually loosening in his jaw. Worried that they might actually come out – and he was proud of his teeth – Graham clamped a hand over his mouth.

I am returning

The wind, swirling around the courtyard, suddenly reversed – not so much a change of direction as a vacuum. The breath was sucked out of everyone – with the exception of Graham, whose eyes bulged with the sudden change in pressure.

'Hang on, everyone!' the Doctor gasped. The flames crackled and spat, clutching at every last bit of oxygen.

Reality warped once more, but this time it felt like a massive convulsion that tore them all out of the shape, out of the universe, out of time itself. In a moment of panic that seemed to last a lifetime, Graham felt himself being drawn away from everyone else, from Ryan, until they were all just tiny, infinitesimal points of light, like stars in the sky.

Then something, everything, blackened like a leaf on a bonfire. The world went into spasm and something bulged through a rent in the universe, glistening like the guts of a hernia.

'Doctor!' Yaz wailed, horrified. 'What's happening?'

'Stay together!' the Doctor yelled. She looked up, around, inside, everywhere – there was no escaping the sight, the sense, of the universal viscera extruding into their reality. Coils slid wetly over one another as something began to unfold on the other side.

'What is it?'

'Reality prolapse,' the Doctor gasped. 'I've opened up a void in the space-time continuum.'

Ryan tried to close his eyes but he could still see the thing, the monstrous entity, swelling straight into his mind. The tips of long, sinuous feelers began to probe into every consciousness within reach.

'It's the Argomeld, isn't it?' Graham realised miserably. 'That's what Zaris is. That's what it looks like.'

The students screamed. Milo swore mightily. Pythagoras staggered.

Somehow the Doctor's voice could be heard over the throb of the emerging Argomeld. 'Stay in position! Keep the shape! It's vital.'

'What's happening?' Yaz's voice rose above the tumult. Clearly she could sense things were getting out of control. And the feeling was spreading.

'The Argomeld's sensed my mind. It can tell it's more advanced – it wants to take me over instead of Myia!'

Ryan's eyes widened. 'I thought we were helping it escape?'

'We're making it worse!' Yaz screamed.

'No we're not,' said the Doctor firmly.

The world around them bulged and slithered, reality warping into a nest of tentacles that reached out for the Doctor.

'That's it … come on, sunshine,' the Doctor said. 'You'll love it in my head. Better view, for a start – on a clear day you can see forever … and the journey back will be *so* much easier!'

The tentacles – invisible, intangible, but clear to everyone in the deepest parts of their consciousness – coiled around the Doctor.

'Stay strong everyone!' cried the Doctor. 'We can do this!'

Graham forced himself to look. The tears were streaming from his eyes. He couldn't tell if he was looking straight into a gale, or the sun, or his own memories. All he could see was the slithering immensity hovering over his world, reaching for the Doctor. He tore his gaze from the nightmare and looked for Ryan.

'Ryan! I'm here, son! Stay strong!'

Ryan's eyes were tight shut, but Graham knew he could still see. 'I'm on it, I'm on it!'

With immense effort, as if he was fighting the g-force of a rocket ship blasting off, Graham raised his free hand and stuck up his thumb.

'Keep together!' the Doctor's voice screamed across the void, at once immeasurably distant and right in his earhole.

Graham struggled to remain exactly where he was, which turned out to be quite difficult as he now felt as though he was hurtling through space like a comet. He was leaving everyone and everything behind, careering into the infinite like the bloke at the end of *2001*. Mercifully, he could no longer see the creature between the dimensions.

'I'm losing it, Doc!' he croaked.

'You're doing fine!' The Doctor's reply, instant and clear, jolted him back to the here and now. He chanced opening his eyes – and saw a maelstrom of rainbow fire, flames of every colour, roaring around him. In the centre of it, arms wide, coat tails flapping in the slipstream, was the Doctor. A bright light shone from her wide open eyes.

'Now's your chance, Zaris!' she cried. 'Go! Leave us alone. Leave *me* alone! Back to your own universe! Back to where you belong!'

And then, with the speed of a slamming door, it was over. The storm abated in a moment, the fires were snuffed out, and everyone was left standing with blackened, smouldering torches. None of them quite knew where they were – except for the Doctor, who was already bounding across the yard to Myia.

Pythagoras's daughter, white as a lily and every bit as weak, collapsed into the Doctor's arms. The Doctor lowered her to the ground as the others crowded around.

'Myia! Daughter!' Pythagoras wiped tears from his eyes as he knelt close. 'For the love of every god, please speak to me.'

'She's going to be fine,' the Doctor said. 'Just give her a minute.'

'But is she all right?' Milo asked. 'Really all right?'

'I'm fine, silly,' Myia said happily, as if she was just waking up from a dream. 'What's been going on? Why do you all look so worried?'

Later, with Myia sitting in the cool of the villa, attended by her husband Milo and every other member of the household who loved her dearly, they asked the Doctor what it was they had seen.

'I don't know,' she confessed. 'A glimpse of something we should never even try to imagine. If you could lift the universe up like a rock in your garden, then maybe that's what you'd find lurking beneath. Something that only exists in the dark. The Argomeld was an extension of it, I think, or perhaps an emissary.'

'It tried to take over your mind, though, Doctor,' said Yaz. 'It could have killed you.'

'It would have done for Myia,' said Graham. 'The Doc was a tougher nut to crack.'

'Big risk to take, though,' Ryan said.

The Doctor's nose wrinkled. 'Nah. Takes more than extradimensional quantum mathematics with an attitude to impress me. I prefer people – the kind who'll stick together and stand up to the monsters. Way more impressive.'

Pythagoras shook the Doctor's hand. 'You taught me this custom, the shaking of the hand,' he told her with a smile. 'It is a good one. My thanks to you once again, dear Doctor.'

'Don't be daft.' The Doctor pulled out her brightest smile. 'Happy to help.'

'I may need to borrow Pythagoras's shades myself, Doc,' said Graham, finishing his last cup of red wine. 'I think this fruity little number has helped my head for now – but I can't vouch for tomorrow morning.'

'Come on, old man,' said Ryan. 'Let's get you to your bed!'

'Before you leave, please ...' Pythagoras offered Graham the leopard-pattern sunglasses. 'I thank you for their use, but they are not mine.'

The Doctor's face crinkled into a frown. 'You sure?'

'Positive.'

'Maybe they *were* Audrey Hepburn's after all,' the Doctor muttered.

Graham perked up a little at this, slipping on the shades and clapping his hands together. 'Right then – nothin' else for it: who fancies a quick trip to Hollywood?'

Mission of the KaaDok

Mike Tucker

The Doctor peered out of the door of the TARDIS and smiled. There were very few places in the universe where the bright blue police box shell of her time machine could go unnoticed. Mid-twentieth-century Britain was one, but the prop store of a major film studio was the other.

She stepped out into the darkened shed. It was perfect. All around there were racks piled high with artefacts from a dozen periods in Earth's history – native American totem poles, Egyptian chariots, 1920s automobiles ... There was even what looked like an egg-shaped spacecraft lurking in one corner. Nestled amongst rows of classical columns, ornate doors and huge Greek-style urns, it was very unlikely that anyone would even give the battered old box a second glance.

'Well, are we there?' came Yaz's impatient voice from over her shoulder.

The Doctor stepped aside and allowed her, Graham and Ryan to tumble out into the jumbled prop room.

'Cool!' Yaz looked around with excitement.

Graham was not so easily impressed. 'Are you sure this is the right place?' he asked, the disappointment evident in his voice. 'Looks a bit grubby ...'

'Definitely the right place,' said the Doctor peering at the readout on her sonic screwdriver. 'Paramount Studios, California, United States of America, January 1961.' She sniffed the air. 'The eighth,' she added solemnly, snapped the sonic device closed and slipped it into the pocket of her jacket. 'Come on.'

Throwing open the doors to the prop room, the Doctor led her friends out into the bright Californian sunshine. As Graham stepped out through the doors, his face lit up. 'Now this is more like it!'

All around them there was bustle and colour. Huge, whitewashed buildings, emblazoned with stage numbers stretched as far as the eye could see, trucks loaded with scenery trundling between them in a seemingly endless procession. People were everywhere, some in suits, some in overalls, some in costumes from as many different periods as the props in the warehouse. Through the crowds raced stressed-looking runners, delivering packages and messages to the various soundstages.

As a couple of young men dressed in sharp pinstriped suits scurried past, deep in conversation, Graham smoothed down the lapels of his jacket. 'Do I look OK? I'm not exactly dressed to meet a movie goddess ...'

Yaz looked at him in amusement. 'It's sweet you're such a big Audrey Hepburn fan.'

'Don't ...' Ryan rolled his eyes. 'Every Christmas, out come the DVDs ... He must have made us watch *My Fair Lady* a million times.'

'Well, that was your Gran's favourite. I always preferred *Breakfast at Tiffany's*.'

'And now here you are about to watch it being filmed!' said the Doctor. 'How brilliant is that!'

'Yeah.' Graham took a deep breath. 'I know.'

'Here.' The Doctor reached into her pocket again and withdrew a large pair of sunglasses. 'You can be the one to give them back to her.'

As Graham took the glasses, Ryan shot him a suspicious glance. 'You're not going to embarrass us, are you?'

'What d'you mean?' asked Graham indignantly.

'Asking for her autograph or something ... Getting all star-struck.'

'Oh, like you wouldn't be if it was that rapper you like. Stormy.'

'Stormzy.'

'Yeah. Him.'

'No.' Ryan shook his head. 'I'd be cool.'

'Oh, yeah right. Like you wouldn't try and get a selfie ...'

'Um, excuse me ...' The Doctor was glaring at them sternly. 'There aren't going to be any selfies. 1961, remember? You know the rules. The only person allowed to use anachronistic technology—'

'Is you!' chimed her three friends simultaneously.

The Doctor grinned. 'Right. Now let's go and return these sunglasses to Audrey Hepburn.'

Graham looked around at the sprawling studio complex. 'We've got to find her first. Where do we start?'

'We ask,' said the Doctor. Locating one of the runners making his way through the crowds, she hurried forward to intercept him. 'Excuse me!'

The boy looked round. 'Yes, miss?'

'I'm wondering if you can help me. We're trying to find out which stage they're filming *Breakfast at Tiffany's*. We've got something for Miss Hepburn.'

'I'm sorry.' The boy shook his head. 'I'm not allowed to pass out information like that to members of the public.'

'Quite right too. But we're not members of the public.' The Doctor pulled her wallet of psychic paper from her jacket pocket and presented it with a flourish. 'Sarah Jane Smith, Senior Managing Director at *Metropolitan Film Magazine*. This is my sales and marketing team, Yaz, Ryan and Graham. We're doing an exclusive editorial feature on the studio.'

The boy stared wide-eyed at the Doctor's virtual credentials.

The Doctor leaned forward conspiratorially. 'We've come over from London, England.'

That, more than anything, seemed to galvanise the boy into action. 'Right, miss. I'll take you right there. Follow me.'

As he set off across the backlot, the Doctor turned and grinned at her three friends. 'Come on.'

The interior of the soundstage was huge, dark and slightly musty smelling. Huge lights hanging from the ceiling illuminated a set of the interior of a New York apartment. Outside of that pool of light, people stood in quiet huddles watching as the director prepared to rehearse his actors.

'That's Blake Edwards,' whispered Graham. 'Looks like they're about to shoot the party scene in Holly's apartment.'

'So what's this film about?' asked Ryan. 'Why do you get so excited about it?'

'Well, Audrey's Holly Golightly, and she's doing some dodgy stuff, and then she meets this new neighbour . . .'

As Graham started to explain the basic plot, the Doctor regarded the director with amusement. With his close-cropped hair, and prominent ears, it was almost like looking back in time . . . A different body. A different Doctor. So long ago . . .

The Doctor was pulled from her reverie by an excited gasp from Graham.

'Oh, good lord, there she is.'

She followed his gaze to where a slim, delicate woman was crossing the studio floor, surrounded by a phalanx of costume and make-up assistants. Immediately, the murmuring conversations fell quiet, and all eyes followed Audrey Hepburn as she made her way to the set. The Doctor was impressed. The ability to bring a room to a standstill like this was a rare gift. It was no wonder she was a star.

Graham watched, entranced, as Audrey Hepburn began to rehearse the scene. Although initially interested, Yaz and Ryan swiftly started to grow impatient as the same actions were rehearsed over and over again, but they both had enough sense to realise that they needed to stay quiet and inconspicuous.

The Doctor looked at the other people waiting quietly in the gloom around the edge of the studio. Bored-looking construction workers stood waiting for the next break in filming, make-up artists sat with bags bulging with cosmetics, ready to hurry onto the set if the need arose, men in suits watched proceedings with stern expressions, cigars clamped between their teeth.

The Doctor was about to return her attention to the filming when movement in the shadows around the edge of the stage caught her eye. A diminutive figure was moving stealthily along the wall, its features shrouded by the hood of its jacket.

Her curiosity piqued, the Doctor slipped away from her friends and began to follow the figure at a distance, determined to get a closer look. Its attention seemed to be directed at the filming going on in the centre of the stage. More specifically, it seemed to be concentrating on Audrey Hepburn.

Reaching a deserted part of the stage, the figure stopped, and the Doctor had to duck behind a cluster of lamps as it looked around warily, obviously checking to see if it was being watched. Then the figure reached inside its hooded jacket, extracted a gleaming, pistol-like device and levelled it deliberately at the movie star.

With horror, the Doctor realised that she was too far away to have any chance of stopping the figure pulling the trigger. Even as she watched, a faint, ethereal beam of energy began to emanate from the tip of the weapon, snaking its way towards the oblivious actress.

As the Doctor looked around frantically for a solution she suddenly noticed several huge black drapes furled up in the studio ceiling. Snatching the sonic screwdriver from her pocket, she set it to maximum and aimed it at the ropes holding the drapes in place. There was a sharp 'crack' as the fibres parted under the onslaught of the sonic vibrations and waves of black cloth tumbled down towards the studio floor.

The drapes hit the floor with a deafening *whumph,* launching clouds of dust into the air, blocking the path of the energy beam and sending the hooded figure tumbling backwards. On the other side of the drape there was pandemonium: furious voices demanding to know what was going on and the sound of stage technicians running to see what had caused the curtains to fall.

Ignoring the chaos she had caused, the Doctor marched towards the small, hooded figure, looming over it.

'Whatever you're planning, it stops now.'

Startled, the figure swung towards her, and as it did so the ghostly, pale beam of energy from the muzzle of the weapon washed over her, making her stagger.

'Doctor?' Yaz and Ryan came running over, alerted by the commotion. 'Are you OK?'

The figure gave a cry of alarm, stuffed the weapon back into its jacket and scrambled to its feet to flee but, despite her swimming head, the Doctor was determined to get some answers.

'Oh no you don't.'

She lunged forward, catching hold of the figure by its hood. With a hiss of displeasure, it started to struggle, strong despite its small size.

'Ryan, give me a hand here!' yelled the Doctor, aware that they needed to get her prisoner out of the studio. 'Yaz, open that fire door.'

With Yaz and Ryan's help, the Doctor managed to bundle the figure out of the door and they emerged into a wide, deserted alleyway behind the stage.

Reaching into the figure's jacket, the Doctor grabbed hold of the gun that it had been using. 'You won't be needing this any more.'

The figure reached desperately for the weapon. 'Please, I need that.' The voice was thin, high-pitched and sounded desperately unhappy.

'Yeah, right.' Ryan pushed it back roughly. 'Well, tough. You can't be going around shooting movie stars.'

'That's odd...' The Doctor was examining the weapon curiously.

'What is it?' asked Yaz.

The Doctor pulled her sonic screwdriver from her pocket, scanned the weapon and looked at the readout in surprise. 'It's not a gun. It's a neurological scanner.' She looked down at the figure curiously. 'What are you scanning Audrey Hepburn with a neurological scanner for?'

Before the figure could answer, the door to the studio crashed open and an annoyed-looking Graham emerged. 'I might have known it was you lot making all that racket. Can't we go anywhere without it turning into a palaver...?' He looked down at the hooded figure. 'Who's this, then?'

The figure pulled back its hood to reveal a smooth, rodent-like face, large purple eyes blinking in the bright Californian sunlight.

'An alien?' Graham's eyes widened in surprise. 'What's an alien doing here?'

'My name is PhiLit,' said the creature in its high-pitched voice. 'I'm a KaaDok. I teleported down to Earth a few hours ago from a ship that is parked in orbit.'

'Of course . . .' The Doctor rolled her eyes. 'I knew that silver egg in the prop store looked familiar. It's a teleport pod!'

PhiLit nodded.

'OK, that explains the "who" and the "how",' said Yaz. 'What about the "why"?'

'I think we'd all like to know that . . .' The Doctor squatted down in front of the creature. 'Care to give us an explanation?'

The creature gave a deep sigh. 'It's really not as sinister as you think. The KaaDok are huge fans of the television and film output of this planet.'

'You're kidding me?' snorted Ryan. 'You're saying you've got Sky or Netflix or something? You're sitting up in your spaceship watching box sets of *Game of Thrones* . . .?'

'No, no, no.' The Doctor shook her head. 'Every transmission, every television show, every radio broadcast, it just beams out into space, year after year, an endless stream of data from the planet Earth, a living history. The KaaDok must be intercepting those signals.'

PhiLit nodded. 'We had nothing like it on our world. Once we discovered the transmissions, we began to intercept more and more of them. We became fascinated by the images from this planet. Now we are your number one fans.'

'I know what you mean.' The Doctor leaned forward conspiratorially, 'I'm not actually from this planet, but I'm a pretty big fan myself.'

'OK. So you're a big fan of our TV and films,' said Ryan, suspiciously. 'Still doesn't explain that, does it?' He pointed at the neurological scanner in the Doctor's hand.

'No ...' The Doctor had to agree. 'It's not exactly the same as asking for an autograph, is it?'

'The scanners allow us to collect copies of brainwave patterns.'

'Us?' queried Yaz. 'There are more of you?'

'Oh yes.' The KaaDok nodded cheerfully. 'There are dozens of us, travelling all through the history of this planet collecting brainwave patterns from hundreds of celebrities.'

'But what for?' asked Graham impatiently.

'For the wax-bots' said PhiLit as if that explained everything. 'For the museum. Miss Hepburn is going to be a very popular addition to the Twentieth Century gallery.'

'Oh, that's brilliant!' The Doctor clambered back to her feet and turned to her friends with a huge grin on her face. 'I've heard of the KaaDok. They've created a Madame Tussauds in space, populated with android replicas of Earth celebrities.'

'Populated?' said Ryan. 'You mean these things move around?'

'Yes. The KaaDok come down here, collect brainwave patterns, then upload them into the androids to create perfect walking, talking wax replicas.' She sighed. 'I'd always hoped that someone would make a waxwork of me one day.' A puzzled look crossed the Doctor's face. 'But wait, hang on a minute. This is a pretty small-scale device to perform a brainwave scan, particularly if you're collecting more than one pattern. I appreciate you're downsizing to avoid any lasting discomfort to those you're scanning, but surely the data will start to deteriorate pretty quickly.'

PhiLit nodded. 'The transfer to the wax-bot's neural mesh has to be done within minutes for it to be successful.'

Yaz frowned. 'But surely that means that you'd have to have the wax replica nearby ...'

'Oh yes,' said PhiLit. 'The replica of Miss Hepburn is on board my transport pod. Would you like to see?'

Before the Doctor could reply, the door to the studio crashed open again, and a furious voice rang out.

'Are you the ones who just ruined the last take? George and I have been rehearsing that scene for hours and that was the best that it had been.'

The Doctor and her friends turned slowly to find Audrey Hepburn glaring at them.

'Oh, blimey,' said Graham, trying to obscure her view of PhiLit.

'Well?' The actress strode towards them, her elfin features creased with anger. 'What have you got to say for yourselves?'

Graham suddenly realised how Henry Higgins must have felt like when confronted by an angry Eliza Doolittle. He did the only thing he could think of.

'Here ...' He pulled the sunglasses from his pocket. 'We just wanted to return these ...'

The Doctor hurried forward to try to explain. 'I'm very, very sorry about that. Needed to create a diversion, didn't really have much time to think ...'

Audrey ignored her, staring at the sunglasses in Graham's hand. 'Those are the glasses that were stolen from me!'

'Stolen?' Graham looked crestfallen.

'Oh!' The Doctor shook her head. 'No no no … Borrowed, perhaps …'

'You stole Audrey Hepburn's sunglasses?' Graham gave a sigh of despair. 'Only you, Doc …'

Sheepishly, the Doctor turned back to her friends. 'I was in my last body at the time. In the Belgian Congo. I'd been tracking a Barroxian surveillance probe that had crashed in the forest near where they were filming. I needed a UV shield to inspect the malfunctioning photon drive, but had left my sonic sunglasses in the TARDIS, and *her* sunglasses were just lying there …'

Audrey was staring at the Doctor curiously. 'It was the night we saw that meteor. There was a tall, grey-haired man who suddenly appeared out of nowhere and—'

She broke off as she suddenly caught a glimpse of the diminutive KaaDok peering up at her from behind Graham's legs.

'Oh my …'

The Doctor sighed. 'Miss Hepburn – Aud – I think we owe you an explanation …'

A short while later, the Doctor, her friends and Miss Hepburn were standing in front of PhiLit's teleport pod: the squat, silver egg, squatting on four stumpy legs, that was standing in the corner of the prop store where the Doctor had landed the TARDIS.

'Concealing our transport is always a matter of some concern,' explained the KaaDok. 'Fortunately, film and television studios have many places such as this that are ideal for our purposes.'

'Yes ...' said the Doctor, glancing over at the battered blue shell of her own transport. 'Lucky that ...'

Audrey was staring at the pod with disdain. 'I don't understand. Surely this is just a prop from that science fiction film that they're filming on the back lot.' A thought suddenly struck her and she glanced down at the KaaDok. 'Yes, of course. You're extras from the film. This is just some practical joke. Blake isn't going to be pleased when he finds out, you know ...'

'It's a little bit more complicated than that,' explained the Doctor. 'PhiLit ...'

PhiLit pushed back the sleeve of his jacket, revealing a complex wrist-device. He pressed a sequence of buttons and there was a sharp crackle as a gleaming, silver teleport pod split open and light flooded out into the prop store.

The Doctor peered into the interior of the pod. A compact control console stood in the centre of the tiny craft and the curved walls were lined with alcoves just big enough to hold a person. One of those alcoves was occupied.

Audrey had spotted the figure too and her eyes opened wide with astonishment. 'I don't believe it ...'

PhiLit reached out for the neurological scanner in the Doctor's hand. 'May I?'

The Doctor handed over the device, watching as PhiLit made a number of delicate adjustments before activating it. The same pale, ghostly light that the Doctor had seen in the studio enveloped the motionless figure in the alcove, and moments later it stepped out of the pod.

Audrey stared in astonishment at her double. The resemblance was quite uncanny. The KaaDok had done an extraordinary job. The features were identical, the build exact … Even the stitching on the costume appeared to have been copied.

'Why isn't it talking?' asked Ryan.

'The neural net will take a little time to get to full autonomic function,' explained PhiLit.

'Well, the other one isn't talking much either,' pointed out Graham, 'and I don't think that's got anything to do with neural nets.'

The Doctor glanced at Audrey, who was obviously struggling to come to terms with what she was seeing. 'Are you OK?'

The simple question pulled the actress from her from her daze. 'What? Yes. This is all a little … unexpected, that's all.' She looked at the Doctor curiously. 'Extraordinary things seem to happen when you are around, Doctor.'

The Doctor shrugged. 'Occupational hazard, I'm afraid.'

'Well, you still owe me an explanation as to what all this –' she gestured to the wax-bot and the waiting PhiLit – 'is all about.'

'The truth?' With a deep breath, the Doctor explained about the KaaDok's peculiar obsession with Earth entertainment, and their mission to collect brain patterns for the exhibits in their wax museums.

'So the work that we do, the films we make, the television shows, are being watched all through the galaxy?'

'Yes.' The Doctor nodded. 'Your work reaches billions of people, of all races.'

'Bet you wish your agent got the repeat fees for all that, eh?' said Graham cheekily.

Ignoring him, Audrey ran her hands over the metallic silver skin of the teleport pod. 'And these aliens – these KaaDok – they travel through space in craft like this?'

'Well, no. This is just a short-range transport pod.'

'Our mother ship is in orbit,' explained PhiLit. 'From there, the Supervisor can beam us down to locations all over the world.'

'Can we see it?' Audrey turned back towards the Doctor, her eyes shining with excitement.

'What?' The Doctor was taken aback. 'You want to go up and see the mothership?'

'Yes.' Audrey nodded. 'Ever since that night in the jungle, I've dreamed about the worlds beyond the stars. I want to see these wonders for myself.'

The Doctor grinned. 'Aud, you are brilliant!'

'Hey, now hang on a minute, Doc.' Graham sounded concerned. 'You can't just go whizzing off into space with Audrey Hepburn!'

'Why not?' said the Doctor and Audrey simultaneously.

'Because she's meant to be making *Breakfast at Tiffany's*!' spluttered Graham. 'It's Elvis all over again. What about ... causality? What about not altering established history? If anything happened whilst you were up there ...'

The Doctor's face fell. 'Yeah, you're right.'

'Oh.' Audrey looked crestfallen. 'Surely just a quick trip can't hurt?'

'I really don't think it's a good idea. We can't be jeopardising the Oscar win now, can we?'

'Oscar?' Audrey's eyes widened even further. 'You don't mean ...?'

'Said too much already, I'm afraid,' said the Doctor firmly. 'Spoilers ...' She turned to her three friends. 'I want you lot to get Audrey back to the set.'

'Why?' asked Ryan. 'Where are you going?'

'Up to the mothership to see PhiLit's Supervisor.' Immediately there were three protesting voices, but the Doctor was having none of it. 'It doesn't need all of us to go. The KaaDok aren't exactly breaking any of the laws of time, but it won't hurt to just give them a friendly, Time-Lordy reminder of their responsibilities as time travellers.'

'I thought *she* was meant to be the police officer,' grunted Ryan, looking at Yaz.

'Well, she's certainly the responsible adult.' The Doctor beamed. 'So she's the one I'm entrusting with my psychic paper.' She pulled the small leather wallet from her jacket pocket and handed it over to Yaz. 'You know how it works ... If you have any problems, this should sort them out.' She turned back to where PhiLit had been busying himself loading the wax-bot of Audrey back into its alcove in the teleport pod. 'Right! One to see the Supervisor, please.'

PhiLit looked at her dubiously. 'That might not be a good idea ... Mr AaRee doesn't like anything that interrupts the routine, and I'm already running late, and—'

'Mr AaRee?'

'My Supervisor.'

'Oh, I'm sure we can straighten everything out with him.' The Doctor scampered on board, settling back into one of the other alcoves and smiling at him expectantly.

Realising that he wasn't going to dissuade her, PhiLit activated the controls on his wrist device and the curved sliver doors of the pod started to close.

The Doctor grinned at her friends. 'See you later!'

Moments later there was a sharp electrical crackle and the pod vanished.

'Well, that's just typical,' said Graham with a sigh. 'She gets to go off and have all the fun whilst we're left here to do all the hard work.'

'Yeah.' Yaz shook her head in despair. 'Because spending time looking after your all-time favourite actress is a real hardship, isn't it?'

Graham looked sheepish, and turned to where Audrey was waiting patiently. 'OK, Miss Hepburn. I guess we'd better get you back on set, hadn't we?'

The actress said nothing.

'Miss Hepburn?' With a horrible sinking feeling, Graham waved his hand in front of her face. There was no reaction whatsoever. 'Oh no …'

'You've got to be kidding me.' Yaz stared at him in disbelief. 'It's the waxwork!'

Graham's smile was rueful. 'Looks like Audrey's got her trip into space with the Doc after all.'

*

The teleport pod materialised in a blaze of crackling energy. Moments later, the hull cracked open and the Doctor and PhiLit stepped out into the cavernous hangar of the KaaDok mothership.

The Doctor looked around and gave a whistle of admiration. 'I'm impressed. I had no idea that this was such a big operation.'

'Oh yes.' PhiLit nodded. 'There are more than forty of us gathering neurological data from over a dozen time zones on this trip alone.'

'How do you decide which celebrities to scan?'

PhiLit frowned. 'It's based on ratings, I think. I do know that Audrey Hepburn has been top of the list of the most requested wax-bots for quite some time.'

'I'm so very pleased to hear that.'

Startled, the Doctor and PhiLit turned to see Audrey looking around at the vast interior of the KaaDok ship. Puzzled, PhiLit glanced at the settings on his neurological scanner. 'That can't be right.'

'Oh no ...' The Doctor's face fell. 'Please tell me you didn't ... Please tell me you didn't switch places with the replica.'

'I most certainly did,' said Audrey stepping out of the teleport pod. 'This is the second time that unexplained events have interrupted my life, Doctor, the second time that I have found myself confronted by things that I barely understand. This time I am determined to see what it is all about first-hand.'

The Doctor opened her mouth to argue, and then thought better of it. 'Ah well.' She shrugged. 'I just hope that your replica remembers its lines.'

Apparently unconcerned by what might be happening back at the film studio, Audrey continued to take in her surroundings. 'So is this where the other replicas are stored?' she asked the anxious-looking KaaDok.

'Yes.' PhiLit nodded. 'Over here.'

The little alien set off towards a hatchway on the far side of the hangar. Audrey and the Doctor followed. As they stepped through the opening, Audrey gave a gasp of astonishment.

'Look at them all!'

The chamber beyond was lined with alcoves similar to the ones on the teleport pod. Hundreds of them, each holding a different film star. Slowly they made their way along one wall, staring up at the ranks of motionless figures. 'Mae West, John Wayne, Oliver Hardy, Gene Kelly ...' The Doctor gave a whistle of awe. 'You've been a busy little KaaDok, haven't you?'

'It's like a *Who's Who* of the entire planet,' exclaimed Audrey.

'Looks like you've got a few gaps, mind you,' said the Doctor, indicating a row of empty alcoves. Each of them was emblazoned with a sticker saying REJECTED. 'Why have these been rejected? And what happens to them when they are?'

PhiLit shuffled uncomfortably. The Doctor had a feeling that his reluctance to divulge what had happened to those particular wax-bots was not good news.

Before she could press him further, a hatchway on the opposite side of the chamber suddenly slammed open, and a large figure heaved itself through.

'PhiLit! What's going on?'

'Oh, good lord!' gasped Audrey as the alien came lumbering towards them. 'What on earth is that?'

PhiLit was cringing, hopping from foot to foot. 'That's my Supervisor.'

The huge KaaDok stared down at them angrily. 'Who the devil are these two? And what are they doing interfering with my cargo!'

'I don't believe it.' Graham had his head in his hands. 'Audrey Hepburn goes off on a jolly with the Doctor and we're left with a robot to finish filming her scenes on one of the most iconic films of all time. What are we going to do?'

'I say we let the machine do its thing,' said Ryan shrugging.

'What?'

'It looks like her, it's got her brainwaves so it presumably thinks like her ... Who's going to know the difference?'

'He's right, you know,' agreed Yaz, peering closely at the motionless wax-bot. 'No one is ever going to know that it's a robot.'

'*I'll* know!' complained Graham. 'I'll never be able to look at that film the same way again. Besides, in case you two haven't noticed, this thing still isn't talking. How's it going to do its scenes if it can't speak?'

'PhiLit did say that it would take a while for it to get going properly,' said Yaz.

'Perhaps there's a switch we need to turn on,' suggested Ryan.

'No!' said Yaz firmly. 'Waxwork or not, we are *not* going to go searching Audrey Hepburn for hidden switches.'

'Perhaps we just need to ask it something,' said Graham, taking a step back. 'All right, cockle? You feeling OK?'

The replica turned towards her and smiled. 'I'm feeling grand, thanks,' it said in a broad Yorkshire accent. 'But I could murder a cup of tea.'

Ryan laughed out loud. 'Genius! A northern Audrey Hepburn!'

'It must be something to do with the Doctor getting in front of that neurological scanner,' said Yaz. 'It's mixed up their brainwaves!'

Graham was practically pulling his hair out. 'Well, we can't stick her in front of the camera sounding like that!'

'This might just be a glitch or something,' said Yaz. 'Let's just get her back onto the stage and hope that she settles down.'

Reluctantly, Graham had to agree; until the Doctor got back with the real deal, there was nothing else they could do. Leaving the prop shed, the three of them led the wax-bot back towards the soundstage, the task made more complicated by the fact that the wax-bot, again like the Doctor more than Audrey, wanted to stop and talk to practically everyone she met. Finally they made it back to the stage, but as Graham ushered the wax-bot through the doorway, Ryan suddenly became aware of someone watching them from the far end of the alleyway. He frowned. He was sure it was someone he recognised.

With a sudden jolt, he realised why the figure's face was familiar and grabbed Yaz by the arm. 'Yaz, look.' He pointed at the figure. 'It's Alan Rickman!'

'What?' Yaz stared at him as if he was mad. 'Don't be daft. We're in Hollywood in the 1960s, remember?'

'I know that, but look!'

Yaz followed Ryan's gaze. The face staring back did indeed seem to be that of Alan Rickman. More than that, it seemed to be Alan Rickman as he had appeared as the Sheriff of Nottingham in *Prince of Thieves*. He was even wearing the robes.

She was about to tell herself that she was being ridiculous when another figure stepped into view, and Yaz realised that she knew this man's face as well.

Ryan recognised him too. 'Oh, my God! It's whatshisname . . . Sherlock! Benedict Cumberbatch!'

Yaz nodded. It was becoming fairly obvious that Audrey Hepburn wasn't the only replica running around the studio backlot.

'Are you two coming or what?' Graham was calling to them impatiently at them from the doorway.

As the two wax-bots turned and walked off, Yaz pulled the Doctor's psychic paper from her pocket. She thrust it into Graham's hands. 'Here, you're probably going to need this.'

'What? Why? Where are you going?'

'There are more wax-bots out here! We've got to follow them, we've got to find out how many of them there are.'

Before Graham had a chance to complain, Yaz and Ryan raced off in pursuit of the replicas.

Back on the spacecraft, the imposing figure of the Supervisor continued to glare down at the Doctor,

Audrey and a trembling PhiLit. 'Well, PhiLit? I'm still waiting for an answer.'

Pulling the terrified little KaaDok to one side, the Doctor stepped forward with her most disarming smile. 'Hi. Mr AaRee, right? Perhaps I can explain. I'm the Doctor. Now, I must admit that I usually have a clever piece of paper for moments like this that would tell you that I'm a really, *really* important person and that you should definitely listen to what I have to say, but I've had to lend that piece of paper to a friend, so perhaps you can just take it as read that I'm really, really important, and listen to what I have to say anyway.'

'What?' AaRee snatched the neurological scanner out of PhiLit's hand and stared at the readout. 'You're not wax-bots, you're organic. What are you doing here?'

'Oh, it's just a flying visit, honest. Miss Hepburn here fancied seeing your spacecraft …'

'Miss Hepburn?' AaRee sounded surprised. 'Audrey Hepburn?'

To her credit, Audrey didn't flinch as the imposing alien leaned down to get a closer look at her. 'Delighted to meet you,' she said calmly. 'I gather I'm becoming quite a celebrity in these parts …'

AaRee was silent for a moment, and then let out a guffaw of laughter. 'Well, well. Wait until the guys hear about this. Audrey Hepburn. On my ship!' He shook his head. 'You're an idiot, PhiLit. You're only meant to get the brainwave pattern, not bring the entire life form.'

'Sorry, Supervisor AaRee.'

'And what have you done with the wax-bot, eh? Left it down there on the planet, I suppose.'

'Yes, it's the location of a few other wax-bots that I wanted to talk to you about, actually,' interrupted the Doctor. 'I couldn't help noticing that you've got a few empty alcoves. Quite like to know what happened to them?'

AaRee grunted. 'Some of the collectors left it too long transferring some of the brainwave patterns. The neural mesh didn't take properly. Once that happens the wax-bot is useless.'

'So you've just dumped them?'

'Sure.'

'Where?'

'Where do you think?'

'Down there? On Earth?' The Doctor was horrified. 'You can't drop tech that sophisticated on Earth at this point in its history.'

AaRee shrugged, obviously unconcerned. 'Look, it's a waste of my time and resources to ship defective 'bots back to KaaDok Major. Plus I have to explain to the management what went wrong and there's a possibility of me having to pay for replacement 'bots. That cuts into my profits.' He glared at PhiLit. 'This lot struggle to get their little heads around that, but I shouldn't really be surprised. They're only children, after all.'

'Hang on a second …' The Doctor frowned. 'Did you say *children*?'

'Yeah? What of it?'

Audrey was appalled. 'Are you telling me that you are using children to do this work for you? It's bad enough that you are happy to exploit *any* worker, but children?'

AaRee rolled his eyes. 'Oh, please. Not another do-gooder. I get enough of this back on KaaDok Major. Look, the transport pods put a lot of strain on a body. The kids stand up better to the process than adults, so I saw an opportunity and I put them to work. They're fine! They get food, lodgings, and a bonus if they hit their targets. It's not like they're slaves, or anything.'

'Oh? I think it's a lot like that …' The Doctor looked down at PhiLit's anxious face, and felt a surge of anger beginning to rise in her. 'And that means that I'm going to have to stop you.'

As Yaz and Ryan trailed the two wax-bots through the studio lot, they began to spot more and more anachronistic figures – so far they'd seen Zoë Ball, Tom Selleck, a young Judy Garland, Bono and little Jimmy Krankie, and half-a-dozen more that neither of them had recognised. Strangely they all seemed to be drawn towards one another, and now there was a cluster of nearly a dozen or so mismatched celebrities wandering aimlessly through the bustling crowds.

'They look a bit mindless, don't they?' said Ryan. 'Like a herd of famous sheep.'

'Yeah.' Yaz nodded in agreement. 'Remember how the Audrey robot just stood there until we spoke to it?'

'Like it was waiting for orders.'

'Exactly.' She thought for a moment. Ryan's analogy of the robots being like sheep was a good one. Perhaps rounding them up might be easier than they thought. 'Maybe all we need to do is tell them to follow us.'

'Follow us where?'

'Back to the TARDIS. Surely they can't do any harm in there and the Doctor can decide what to do with them once she gets back.'

Ryan nodded. 'Sounds good. Let's do it ...'

Before they could try their plan, a voice rang out across the backlot. 'Oi! You lot ...'

In unison all the wax-bots turned to face a man with a bullhorn who was glaring at them.

'Did you all get lost? You should have been on set ages ago!' He gestured at them angrily. 'Come on! This film isn't going to make itself, you know!'

The robots began to follow the man, disappearing around the corner of a soundstage.

'Looks like you were right, Yaz,' said Ryan ruefully. 'They were just waiting for orders.'

'Yeah. And now they've got some. Come on we'd better get after them!'

The two of them hurried after the gaggle of robots but, as they rounded the corner, Yaz's heart sank. The robots were being ushered onto an expansive street set, crowded with technicians, actors, lights and cameras. From the look of things, this was the science fiction film that Audrey had mistakenly assumed PhiLit was part of.

The man with the bullhorn was positioning the wax-bots into a larger group of supporting artists, hurrying them along impatiently. Yaz and Ryan edged closer to try and hear what instructions he was giving them.

'Let's join them,' said Yaz suddenly.

'You what?' Ryan stared at her in astonishment.

'It's our best shot at keeping an eye on things. Besides, if we don't look as though we're part of this shoot, then eventually someone is going to spot us and chuck us out.'

Before Ryan could argue, Yaz set off towards the waiting robots. Reluctantly Ryan followed her and the two of them joined the back of the crowd of extras.

'Right, now everybody listen!' yelled the man with the bullhorn. 'The scene that we are about to shoot is the one just after the Zargons have landed.' He indicated half a dozen actors clad in bright silver suits with mirrored visors and holding chunky-looking ray guns that were standing at the far side of the set. 'The Zargon commander is using his mind-controlling ray on you, so when I call "action", I want you do exactly what we rehearsed yesterday. The stunt team playing the soldiers are the enemy. Have you got that? I want perfectly choreographed mayhem. Good, now first positions everyone!'

Ryan grimaced. 'I've got a really bad feeling about this ...'

Yaz was horrified. 'You think that robots are going to take him literally?'

Before they could even begin to think about what they were going to do next, a single word boomed from the bullhorn.

'Action!'

Initially, it wasn't that obvious that anything was wrong. Yes, there were screams and shouts from the set, but the crew looking on were unconcerned, and the director and cameraman seemed more than pleased with what they were getting. It was only when that chaos started to spill off the set that it started to become obvious that something was very, very wrong.

Pushing a cameraman to one side, two of the robots grabbed hold of one of the heavy camera dollies and effortlessly heaved it onto its side, sending the camera itself clattering to the ground. Another robot hurled its weight against a lighting stand and it started to topple. Yaz and Ryan rushed forward, yelling at the shocked crew. 'Look out!'

Jolted into movement, the crew scattered just as the heavy lamp came crashing to the floor, sparks and broken glass exploding everywhere.

The screaming and shouting suddenly took on a different intensity as it became clear that what was unfolding was not part of the filming. People started to run for shelter as the robots began to wreck anything they could get their hands on. Yaz and Ryan did try their best to stop them, their actions finally galvanising other members of the crew to help, but the robots brushed them off with such casual ease that further attempts at quelling the unrest swiftly evaporated.

'This is getting out of control!' Ryan groaned. 'We need the Doctor back here. She'd be able to sort this out with her sonic or something ...'

'Or something ...' An idea suddenly popped into Yaz's head. 'Come on!'

She ran from the set, Ryan racing after her.

'What are you doing. We can't just run away!'

'The psychic paper!' yelled Yaz

'Eh?'

'Look, these robots are effectively a blank slate, right? Obeying any order that they're given. Well, the Doctor's psychic paper sort of reprograms the brain, doesn't it? Makes you see what you think you *should* see.'

'So?'

'Well if the robots are so susceptible to suggestion then it might give us some sort of control over them.'

'But you gave the paper to Graham, remember?'

'Yeah, I know,' said Yaz. 'So I'm going to get it.'

'You?' AaRee stared down at the Doctor in disbelief. 'You're going to stop me?'

'Actually,' Audrey stepped up to the Doctor's side. '*We're* going to stop you.'

'And how are you going to do that, exactly?' sneered the KaaDok Supervisor.

'Like this ...'

The Doctor reached into her jacket and whipped out her sonic screwdriver, but AaRee was too fast for her. Raising the neurological device he fired it at the Doctor, who was immediately engulfed in the ghostly, flickering white light. She clutched her head in agony, the sonic slipping from her fingers and clattering to the deck.

'Supervisor! No!' PhiLit lunged forward to try and stop him, but AaRee swept him aside, sending him crashing against the wall.

'This device is designed to take a copy of an individual brain pattern, Doctor,' snarled AaRee. 'But it is equally capable of removing a brain pattern completely.'

He adjusted the controls, and the beam of light crew brighter. Helpless in the beam, the Doctor gave a cry of agony.

'Enjoy a mindless future, Doctor. Wandering around those movie sets below with the other rejects till you're thrown in the gutter …'

Suddenly the air was filled with a high-pitched warble and the shining cocoon of light surrounding the Doctor started to pulse and flicker.

'What?' growled AaRee, shaking the neurological scanner. 'What is wrong with …?'

Before he could finish his sentence, there was a sharp, deafening crack, and the beam of light seemed to fold back on itself, vanishing from around the Doctor and enveloping the KaaDok Supervisor instead.

The Doctor looked up in astonishment to see Audrey, her elfin features set in an expression of grim determination, wielding the sonic screwdriver as if she'd been born holding it.

With a bellow of rage and pain, AaRee tried to shut off the device, but it was no use. Trapped in the ever-brightening bubble of light he sank slowly to his knees.

As the KaaDok Supervisor collapsed face down on the deck, Audrey shut down the sonic and gave a satisfied nod. 'There. No point in draining his brainwaves completely. We merely want to incapacitate him, not leave him mindless, despite the fact that it was what he intended for you.'

The Doctor scrambled to her feet. 'What did you do?' she asked in amazement.

'I reversed the polarity of the neuron flow,' said Audrey matter-of-factly. She frowned. 'I'm not entirely sure why I should know how to do that, but it seemed like the obvious solution.'

The Doctor grinned. 'I have a feeling that me getting into the path of the beam when PhiLit was scanning your brainwaves might have mixed things up a little.'

'PhiLit!' Suddenly remembering the blow that the little KaaDok had taken, Audrey hurried over to where he was sitting dazed against the wall. 'Oh, you poor thing.'

She helped him to his feet, and the Doctor gave him a quick examination. 'No bones broken. You'll have a bit of a bump on your head, but you'll be fine.'

'What happened?' asked PhiLit, looking in astonishment at the motionless body of his Supervisor slumped on the floor.

'You got a promotion!' said the Doctor cheerfully. 'Until you get back to KaaDok Major, you're the new Supervisor!'

'What are we going to do with him?' Audrey nodded at AaRee.

The Doctor glanced across at the empty alcoves where the wax-bots had been stored. 'I think we should be able to squeeze him into one of those, don't you?'

It was one of the most toe-curlingly embarrassing hours of his life that Graham could ever remember. In fact, he couldn't imagine that there would ever be another hour that would be able to top it.

The Doctor had been completely correct in her supposition that no one on the production would be able to tell the wax-bot Audrey and the real Audrey apart; that part of the plan had been fine. The problem was the way that the wax-bot was acting …

The Doctor's psychic paper had done its job in ensuring that no one questioned Graham's presence alongside her (although from the looks that he was getting from some of the crew he had to wonder what their subconscious minds had written on the blank parchment) and he was confident that he knew the film well enough to get the wax-bot to do what it should be doing in the scene that they were rehearsing.

The problem was, it kept improvising …

In the last half-hour, it had brought filming to a standstill on at least half a dozen occasions, either by suggesting that it might be nice to do a little dance, or juggle, or play the spoons. On the few occasions that she *had* got through the scene as directed, her dialogue had been peppered with so many broad Northern phrases that the director had eventually given up and called an extended tea break.

Graham could see him deep in conversation with a huddle of studio executives on the far side of the studio, and he was now such a deep shade of puce that Graham figured that there was a fair chance that he might literally explode.

He sighed. The only mercy was that the scene that they were meant to be filming was of a raucous party. He shuddered to think how things might have turned out if they had been in the middle of filming one of the more sensitive scenes.

Audrey, or rather the replica Audrey, was standing next to the tea trolley trying to engage George Peppard in conversation about whether they should do the next take wearing fezzes. Graham honestly didn't know how much more of it he could take, so when Yaz came racing across the studio floor towards him he actually felt relieved.

'Graham, she panted. 'Please tell me you've still got the psychic paper ...'

'Of course I have,' he said, pulling the wallet from his pocket. 'Why? What do you need it for?'

'Would you believe a robot uprising?'

Graham stared at her for a moment. 'Right. Better lead on, then ...'

As they hurried towards the studio doors, Ryan glanced back over at the robot Audrey. 'What about her? Are we all right leaving her here on her own?'

Graham nodded wearily. 'Believe me, there's nothing she can do that's any worse than what she's already done.'

The instant that they emerged into the bright Californian sunshine, they could tell that things had become more serious. A dark pall of smoke had begun to rise above the backlot and, in the distance, the sound of sirens could be heard.

Ryan grimaced. 'That's not good. If the police discover that they're robots ...'

Yaz nodded, remembering what the Doctor had said about anachronistic technology when they had landed.

They hurried towards the backlot, pushing through the crowds of people fleeing from the rampaging wax-bots. They arrived back onto the set to find that it had been completely wrecked. Lamps and cameras lay strewn everywhere but, to Yaz's huge relief, there were no bodies visible amongst the wreckage.

The wax-bots were still following their instructions to cause mayhem and were currently on the far side of the set tearing down sections of scenery.

'Blimey,' said Graham. 'They've made a mess, haven't they?'

'Well,' Yaz urged him forward, 'stop them!'

Nervously, Graham edged forward, the psychic paper held in his outstretched hand. 'Oi!' he yelled. 'You lot!'

The robots turned to stare at him.

'Why don't you come over here and have a look at this?'

One by one the wax-bots stopped what they were doing and began to converge on Graham.

'Blooming heck ...' He swallowed hard. 'This had better work ...'

The teleport pod materialised with a sharp *crack*, and the Doctor hopped down out of her alcove, stretching her jaw to try and get her ears to pop. AaRee had been right about one thing: KaaDok transmat was not the smoothest way to travel. She would have to suggest some improvements that could be made to the technology before PhiLit and the others made their return journey to KaaDok Major.

It had taken all three of them to bundle AaRee into one of the alcoves back on the mothership, and the Doctor had then sealed it using her sonic screwdriver. The last thing that she wanted was the Supervisor escaping before PhiLit and the others got home. PhiLit had already sent an emergency transmission back to his home planet and an investigative team was being dispatched to meet them.

Audrey was concerned. 'Do you think the poor things will be all right?'

'They will now …' The Doctor nodded. 'I hacked into AaRee's log and uncovered all sorts of proof of dubious practices that I attached to PhiLit's report. I imagine that PhiLit and the others are going to be in for quite a bit of compensation. Now we just need to round up those missing wax-bots and get you back onto set so you can finish filming *Breakfast at Tiffany's*!'

As PhiLit operated the door controls and the curved walls of the pod curled open, a dozen faces turned to greet them and there was a chorus of voices. 'Hello, Doc!'

The Doctor looked around in astonishment at the crowd of celebrities that was milling around the prop room. 'O-kaaaay …' She spotted Yaz, Ryan and Graham on the far side of the room smiling at her sheepishly. 'Anyone want to explain?'

'Sort of my fault, I guess,' admitted Graham. 'Kind of underestimated how that psychic paper of yours might work.'

Yaz hurried over and explained what had happened on the backlot.

The Doctor sighed. 'So you thought you'd use the psychic paper to bring them back under your control.'

'You should have seen it,' said Ryan, obviously finding it all very funny. 'He just marched onto the set, held up the paper, and told all the robots that they needed to do everything he said.'

'The thing is,' said Graham, 'they didn't stop at taking orders, they started copying everything. What I did, what I said …'

'It's like having a dozen Grahams!' Ryan laughed.

The Doctor nodded. 'Yeah, well, the psychic paper is designed to operate on an organic psyche. The neural net in the wax-bots got overloaded. They've basically taken a complete personality copy.'

'But you can fix it, right?' Graham was obviously not keen on having a dozen robots impersonating him.

'Yeah, I can fix it.'

A sudden frown crossed the Doctor's brow, and she looked around the crowded room. 'Where's the Audrey wax-bot?'

'Still on set.' Graham grimaced. 'There's a bit of a problem with that to tell you about too …'

'Problems! Brilliant. You can tell me on the way over there.' She turned to Audrey. 'I think we'd better get you back on set.'

Audrey nodded. 'I think you're right.'

The Doctor pulled the sunglasses from her pocket. 'Here.'

Audrey shook her head. 'You keep them. You've given a little bit of yourself to me, these can be my gift to you.'

The Doctor smiled. 'I think there's a fair bit of you in me already.' She turned to the waiting wax-bots. 'Right, you lot. Into the teleport pod. I think it's time PhiLit teleported you back to the mothership so that you can get fixed.'

The wax-bots nodded in unison. 'Too right, cockle.'